THERE'S NOTHING
TO BE AFRAID OF

THERE'S NOTHING TO BE AFRAID OF

Marcia Muller

ST. MARTIN'S PRESS
NEW YORK

Library of Congress Cataloging in Publication Data

Muller, Marcia.
    There's nothing to be afraid of.

    I. Title.
PS3563.U397T48   1985   813'.54   85–10903
ISBN 0-312-79955-1

First Edition

10 9 8 7 6 5 4 3 2 1

For Suzanne Rampton

THERE'S NOTHING
TO BE AFRAID OF

— 1 —

San Francisco's Tenderloin is a twenty-square-block district that contains some of the greatest contrasts in the city. One of these confronted me as soon as I got out of my parked car one sunny December morning: a street preacher in baggy pants, stocking cap, and signboards, setting up in front of the Sensuous Showcase Theatre. Down the sidewalk came another study in opposites: schoolchildren, ten or twelve of them, who parted ranks for a slow-moving old bag lady as they ran for a Muni bus. The woman was intent on the trash in the gutter and didn't even look up as the kids—chattering and yelling in what had to be Vietnamese—surged around her. I watched them clamber aboard the bus, then put my keys in my shoulder bag and started off down Eddy Street.

It was funny, I thought, how much this part of the city had changed without my really observing it. The last time I'd worked a case down here—over three years ago—I hadn't seen many children on the streets. The Tenderloin was the refuge of the poor, the disabled, the disturbed, and the vicious; parents hadn't allowed their offspring to wander unattended. But then had come the great influx of Southeast Asian refugees, people with little money and many dreams. And the character of the area had begun to alter, slowly.

Now many of the storefronts were spruced up and offered produce and Oriental groceries. Hole-in-the-wall restaurants bore names such as Saigon Palace and Vientiane West. Dingy hotels were made more cheerful by the presence of plants on the windowsills and fire escapes. And everywhere were the children—being pushed in their strollers, playing on the sidewalks, running in and out of stores. True, the pimps were still here, as well as the pros-

1

titutes and drug pushers and purveyors of pornography. But an uneasy truce had been negotiated between them and the newcomers that permitted all to live in a prickly sort of peace. And the city had even gone so far as to build a playground not far from here on Jones Street.

The place where I was headed was called the Globe Apartment Hotel, a narrow, dark brick structure I spotted midway down the block. It was six stories tall with bay windows jutting out on either side of a central fire escape. Someone had festooned the iron railings with tattered green garlands and red Christmas ornaments that had lost most of their glitter. I took a piece of paper from my jacket and rechecked the address, then went into the lobby.

At one time this had evidently been a regular hotel, because there was a registration desk to the right with pigeonholes in the wall behind it. The holes were empty now and the desk unmanned, although the resident with the case of Christmas spirit had struck here too. A plastic tree, garish green and three feet high, sat on the desk; it was decorated with the same kind of wornout ornaments as the fire escape. Several brightly wrapped packages lay on a white cotton skirt underneath it.

It seemed like a big risk, leaving Christmas presents in the unlocked lobby of a Tenderloin hotel. I went over and picked one of them up; it was light, and shaking it produced no rattle. Just as I was about to set it down, the front door opened. I started guiltily and turned.

The woman who stood there was tall, about five-ten, and must have weighed two hundred pounds. A sacklike dress in red-and-white stripes fell in billowy folds from the enormous shelf of her bosom, and in her unruly gray hair was a corsage of holly and red carnations. This, I thought, had to be Mother Christmas.

She said, "There's nothing in them."

Quickly I replaced the package, smoothing the cotton out around it. "I didn't think there would be, but I was curious. I had to check."

"And if there had been—then what?"

"I'd have put it back."

2

"Yeah?" She folded her arms and regarded me sternly.

I was used to being taken for many things, but never a thief who would stoop so low as to steal someone's Christmas present. "Look," I said, "I was just being nosy."

"Everyone is." She closed the door and came toward me, seeming to fill the tiny lobby. "Since I'm here, can I help you?"

"Uh, yes." As a rule, I'm not easily intimidated, but all that fat seemed to convey authority. I fumbled in my pocket and produced the paper I'd consulted earlier. "I'm here to see Mrs. Lan. The Refugee Assistance Center sent me."

She ignored the paper. "You mean Mrs. Vang."

"I'm sorry?"

"The last name's Vang. You've got it backwards."

"Oh." I looked at the paper again. There, in my boss's bold script, was the name "Mrs. Vang Lan."

"Vietnamese names all sound alike to Westerners," the woman said. "They don't take the trouble to get them right."

Feeling a little defensive—after all, it wasn't even *my* mistake—I said, "Well, I suppose our names all sound alike to them."

"Probably." Then she smiled a big, gap-toothed grin, to let me know she wasn't really hostile. "You must be the detective from the legal service. Lan said the Center told her they would send someone over."

She'd probably guessed who I was all along. "Right. Sharon McCone."

"Sallie Hyde." She held out a big hand that completely engulfed mine. "I live across from the Vangs. Come on, I'll take you up there." She squeezed around me and waddled toward the elevator at the back of the lobby.

Between the two of us, we filled the little cage. Sallie Hyde slammed the iron grille, punched the button for the fourth floor, and the elevator wheezed upward. I glanced anxiously at the certificate posted above the control panel to see when it had last been inspected.

"Don't worry, it won't fall," my companion said. "It's

3

been days since it even got stuck between floors."

I smiled thinly and watched the buttons light up—two, three, then four. There the cage came to such an abrupt halt that it bounced up and down several times.

"At least it has good brakes," I said.

"Works better than anything else in this building." Sallie Hyde yanked on the iron grille, pushed down the lever on the heavy outer door, and ushered me into a narrow, dim hallway.

I'd been in other Tenderloin hotels; this one was different. All the light bulbs worked, the worn green linoleum squares on the floor looked clean, and the paler green walls appeared to have been recently washed. The underlying smell was the usual harsh odor of disinfectant, but those overlaying it were not typical: garlic, fish, and something spicy like hot red peppers. I followed Sallie's red-and-white-striped girth to the right, where a red Exit sign glowed at the end of the hall. She knocked on a door midway between it and the elevator.

The woman who greeted us was around five feet tall and wore a shapeless flowered cotton dress and rubber shower thongs on her feet. Her face was round and plump, and her short black hair was parted in the center and tucked behind her ears. She looked from me to Sallie Hyde, then back over her shoulder into the apartment.

Sallie said, "Hello, Lan. This is Sharon McCone, the lady from the legal service."

Lan Vang smiled and motioned for us to enter. I stepped forward first and was confronted by a sea of faces. There were about ten people in the small room, ranging in age from Mrs. Vang—who must have been around forty—to a baby crawling on the floor. They looked expectantly at me, and then one of them stood.

"Thanks for coming, Sharon." It was Carolyn Bui, a Eurasian woman—half Vietnamese, half American—whom I had met while on a case the previous spring. Shortly afterward, she had been appointed director of the Refugee Assistance Center, a nonprofit organization that aided Southeast Asian refugees in getting settled in their new

4

city. Partly because of her connection with me and partly because of All Souls' low rates for nonprofit groups, she had brought the Center's legal work to the cooperative where I am staff investigator.

"It's good to see you again," I said, clasping her hand.

Carolyn glanced at the door, where Sallie Hyde still stood. The fat woman was surveying the assemblage, obviously realizing there was no way she could squeeze into the already crowded room. Before Carolyn could speak, Sallie said to me, "You need anything, I'm right across the hall. It's my day off, so I'll be home." Then she turned and lumbered off. Lan Vang shut the door, and I immediately began to feel claustrophobic.

I turned back to Carolyn. She said, "I see you've met Miss Hyde."

"Yes. She's . . . quite something."

"A nice lady. She works in a flower stand down at Union Square, and when she's not doing that, she plays surrogate mother to everyone in the building."

As she spoke, I studied Carolyn's delicate oval face, framed by curving wings of shoulder-length hair. She'd been through some rough times in the past year, and the last time I'd seen her, she had been too thin and had looked strained. Now, however, she'd gained weight and there was some sparkle in her eyes. Life must be looking up for her, and I was glad.

"Speaking of everyone in the building," I said, "are they all here in this room?"

She laughed and said something in Vietnamese to Mrs. Vang, who laughed too. "Hardly. You are looking at the Vang family, minus Mr. Vang, who is at work."

"What! They don't all live . . ." I motioned around us. The room—clean, but sparsely furnished—was no more than twelve-by-fourteen. A couch, where Carolyn had been sitting, held three young women, and the rest of the family members perched on its arms or sat on the floor.

"It's a two-bedroom apartment," Carolyn said. "And they make do."

Quickly I counted noses. Eight people, including the

baby—and the absent Mr. Vang made nine. Suddenly my little five-room earthquake-relief cottage seemed palatial.

Carolyn was watching me. "In Saigon," she said, "the Vangs lived in a large house, Mr. Vang owned a wholesale food business, and the children attended private schools. The family fled their homeland in the final hours of the Republic, losing everything. Now they are starting over."

I glanced at Lan Vang and the others. They were listening intently. "What does Mr. Vang do now?"

"The *family* owns a small café on Taylor Street—Lan's Garden, after Mrs. Vang. All who are able work there; in addition, the children go to school or college. Everyone contributes, and they are hoping to one day buy a home in the Sunset District."

The tone of Carolyn's voice and her careful phrasing told me far more than just the outward circumstances of the Vang family. They said, *These are valuable people, and they are not looking for sympathy or charity. They had a great deal once, and they will again.*

Ashamed of my initial condescending reaction, plus the fact that Carolyn and I were speaking as if the Vangs weren't there, I said, "I'd appreciate it if you'd introduce me to everyone."

She nodded and turned to Mrs. Vang. "You've already met Lan Vang, head of the household in her husband's absence."

Mrs. Vang shook my hand formally.

"On the couch," Carolyn went on, "are her daughters—easier to give you the American names they have chosen for themselves—Amanda, Susan, and Dolly."

The young women nodded in unison. They were in their mid-to-late teens and dressed in jeans and sweaters—typical girls.

"Next to Amanda," Carolyn said, "is Duc Vang."

A young man in his early twenties with an odd brushy haircut regarded me solemnly.

"Hello, Duke," I said, thinking incongruously of John Wayne.

6

Duc must have heard the shade of difference in the way I pronounced the name, because he said, "It is D-u-c. Many people think I have taken an American name until they see it spelled out."

Carolyn pointed at the other end of the couch, where a chubby boy of ten or eleven perched on the arm. "Next is Billy Vang."

Billy screwed up his face and grinned hideously. Behind me, his mother made a hissing sound.

"Billy's the family comedian," Carolyn said. "Now we come to those on the floor. The baby is Renee, and next to her is Jenny."

Jenny was about Billy's age and just as plump. She exhibited better manners by smiling prettily.

Carolyn turned to me. "So there you have the entire family. Everyone has stayed home today because this is a vital conference."

"I see."

"In the Vietnamese culture, the family is important. Everyone has a say in decisions and everyone supports the others in times of trouble. Naturally it is necessary they all be here—except for Mr. Vang, who must keep the restaurant open."

Duc stood abruptly. "I will get Miss McCone a chair." He left the room and returned quickly with a straight-backed chair and placed it next to me. "Please," he said, indicating it.

I sat, and Carolyn squeezed onto the couch next to Dolly. She said, "We discussed how to go about this, and decided Mrs. Vang will outline the problem. The others will help when appropriate. Everyone speaks good English, but I'm here to interpret in case there's some difficulty with shades of meaning."

I nodded. Carolyn, I thought, had already done her fair share of interpreting, explaining the family in the context of its culture while appearing to be making only polite introductions.

Mrs. Vang had remained standing by the door; now she

7

dropped gracefully to the floor, folding her legs to one side. The baby, Renee, gave a gurgle and began crawling toward her. Lan Vang held out her hands and drew the child to her as she began to speak in careful, accented English.

"There is bad trouble in this hotel, and my family has been . . ." She paused, looked at Carolyn, then plunged ahead on her own. "We have been elected by the others here to have something done."

After she was silent for a moment, I also looked to Carolyn for guidance. She spoke quickly in Vietnamese, and Lan Vang went on.

"The trouble is that someone seeks to frighten us. There are noises in the basement, where the furnace is. Strange noises. And shadows in the stairwell. And the lights go out."

"Power failures," Carolyn said.

"Yes, power failures. People are caught in the elevator and cannot get out."

I remembered Sallie Hyde's remark that the elevator hadn't gotten stuck between floors in days. "When did these things start?"

Lan Vang glanced at her son Duc. He said, "About a month ago. At first it was noises. We thought perhaps it was something wrong with the furnace. Then the power began to fail. PG and E finally came to investigate and said someone was turning it off at the main switch."

"Can you describe the noises in the basement?"

"Groaning. Howling. It was as if a wild animal was imprisoned there."

"Did anyone go down and look?"

"The manager. Myself and my friends from floor six, the Dinh brothers. We saw nothing."

"All right," I said, taking out a pad and pencil and beginning to make notes, "what about these 'shadows in the stairwell'? What are they like?"

Lan Vang said, "Large, strange shadows. Oddly shaped. They wait for the children and frighten them."

"Can you describe them a little more?"

She glanced at Billy, the chubby little boy on the arm of

the couch, and spoke in Vietnamese. Billy sat up straighter and seemed to swell with importance. "I saw them. Twice. Jenny saw them too."

The little girl nodded solemnly.

"Was there one shadow? Or more than one?" I asked.

"Only one each time."

"What did it look like?"

"Big." He spread his arms wide above his head.

"Big, like people are big?"

"No."

"Like an animal?"

"No . . ." He looked crestfallen, then brightened. "Maybe like an elephant."

Oh, terrific, I thought. An escapee from the zoo is stalking the Tenderloin. "Billy, where did you see the shadow?"

He gave me an exasperated look. "Mama said, in the stairwell."

"*Where* in the stairwell?"

Billy frowned.

From the floor, Jenny said, "On the wall."

I looked down at her. "Did it move?"

"Yes. At first it was standing still. Then it danced around and went up, around the turn to the next floor."

"Did you follow it?"

"No!"

"What did you do?"

"Screamed and got Mama. She came and looked, but by then it was gone."

"Thank you, Jenny."

Obviously proud at having stolen her brother's place in the limelight, Jenny turned to Billy and stuck out her tongue. This one was not as angelic as she had first seemed.

I looked back at Lan Vang. "Mrs. Vang, what about those times the elevator got stuck? Was that during the power failures?"

"Yes, then. But also other times. For no reason, it stopped between floors. Once Mrs. Dinh, who is pregnant, was inside. We feared for the unborn child."

"Did anyone come out to inspect the elevator?"

"No. The manager asked the owner to send someone, and he said he would. But no one came."

I said to Carolyn, "What about this owner?"

"That's another story. I'll fill you in later."

I paused. "Did anyone contact the police about all these things?"

Mrs. Vang said, "There is a foot officer—"

"Beat officer," Carolyn corrected her.

"Yes, beat officer. A Patrolman Sanders. I spoke with him and he came into the hotel and looked around. But he also saw nothing. He said he could do no more unless someone was hurt or if there was proof of what I told him about. He was very nice, but he could not help."

I looked down at the scribblings in my notebook, wondering how seriously the officer had taken Mrs. Vang's complaint and if he'd filed a report on it. "Well," I said, "what I'd like to do now is get a list of the disturbing events, by date."

Lan Vang set the baby in Jenny's lap and rose. She went to a little table next to the couch and took a paper from its drawer. Handing it to me, she said, "We have written it all down."

I unfolded the paper and saw a chart, printed in a neat hand. It contained two columns, respectively labeled Date and Incident. The first entry was for November 17, and it read, "Jenny Vang frightened by howling in furnace room. Mrs. Zemanek goes down, says no one there."

"Who's Mrs. Zemanek?" I asked.

"The manager," Carolyn said. "We'll see her later."

"Okay." I glanced over the list again, pleased at its detail. If only all my clients were so well prepared. "I think what I should do is study this list, check around, and then get together with all of you again when I have further questions. Would this evening be convenient?"

Lan Vang said, "It will have to be very late. We must be at the restaurant until after eleven."

I thought of my evening's plans. My boyfriend, Don Del Boccio, was coming to my house for dinner, but then he

10

had a taping scheduled at the radio station where he was a disc jockey. I would be left to my own devices from about nine o'clock on. "That's all right," I said. "I'm used to late hours too."

"Thank you, Miss McCone." Lan smiled for the first time, a shy and somewhat tremulous smile that made me determined to help her and the other residents if I could. Then her eyes clouded and she clasped her roughened hands to her breasts. "I hope you can do something for us. It is so frightening."

Carolyn spoke soothingly to her in Vietnamese.

Lan Vang looked at her and said, "I know; that is what Sallie Hyde is always telling us. 'There is nothing to be afraid of.' I wish I could believe it is so."

— 2 —

Carolyn and I said goodbye to the Vangs and walked silently toward the elevator. When their door had closed and we were out of earshot, I said, "How serious do you think this problem is?"

"Serious enough that I'm willing to spend the Center's money to have you investigate it. These are not fanciful people; they've experienced real danger in their lives, and they don't imagine things. I think someone's trying to frighten them for some reason, and I want to put a stop to it."

I nodded and looked up and down the hall, trying to get a sense of how the hotel was laid out. At the end where the Vangs' apartment was, the Exit sign glowed over a door that presumably opened into the stairwell where the frightening shadows lurked. At the other end, ahead of us, a window opened onto an airshaft; through it I could see

11

the grimy stone wall of the building next door. Four doors opened off the hallway on the side that fronted on Eddy Street, but only two on the wall opposite. The front apartments were probably one-bedrooms or studios, while those in the rear—one of which was the Vangs'—would be two-bedrooms. The elevator was in the center of the building, midway between the two rear apartments.

Carolyn punched the elevator button and said, "I think you should meet the manager, Mrs. Zemanek, and then look the building over."

"Okay. But before we see her, tell me something about Mrs. Zemanek."

"There's really not much to tell." The elevator arrived, its door opening about three inches and stopping there. Carolyn sighed and flung it all the way open, then wrestled with the iron grille. "No wonder it gets stuck between floors." She waved me into the cage, then said, "Anyway, about Mary Zemanek. She's a lady of around seventy who supplements her Social Security with this job. I don't think it pays much, but it does include a free apartment. Mrs. Zemanek seems to genuinely care for most of the tenants, and she doesn't exhibit hostility toward the Vietnamese—which is something we're up against all the time in these Tenderloin hotels—but she tends to side with the owner if there's any sort of dispute."

The elevator bumped to a stop at the ground floor. "Have there been many?"

"A fair number. Like I said, Mrs. Zemanek needs the job to supplement her Social Security payments, and she's not about to make any waves."

Carolyn led me from the elevator to a door next to the deserted reception desk. "Mrs. Zemanek's apartment." She knocked and seconds later it was opened by a small woman whose short white hair was arranged in tight snail-like curls. She looked at Carolyn, and then her pale blue eyes surveyed me from head to foot.

"So you're planning to go ahead with this foolishness," she said in a low-pitched voice that was gravelly with age.

"If you mean that I'm going to get to the bottom of what's been happening here, yes." There was an edge to Carolyn's words; I gathered she'd had trouble with the manager before.

"The owner won't like somebody snooping around on his property."

"The owner will like it less if something really bad happens here."

The little woman stood her ground, blue-veined hand on the doorknob. "Is this the detective?" She jerked her tightly curled head at me.

"Yes, this is—"

"What if something happens to her?"

"Like what?"

"What if she falls on the stairs? Or gets hurt prowling around in the basement? This is an old building; plenty of things can happen. The owner wouldn't like—"

"The owner has insurance to cover things like that. Besides"—Carolyn glanced at me, faint amusement in her eyes—"Ms. McCone has been a detective for many years. She can take care of herself."

Mary Zemanek looked doubtful. "It's a funny job for a woman. I'd feel better if you'd brought a man."

"Well, it can't be helped."

"The owner wouldn't—"

"Mrs. Zemanek." Carolyn raised her voice a little. "I would like your permission for Ms. McCone to look over the building."

"What if I refuse?"

"That, of course, is your right. But if she's denied access, we might have to call the police in to investigate instead. You can't refuse to let *them* on the premises."

A look of guile came into the old lady's pale eyes. "The police were here before and they didn't find anything."

"They can always come back again. And this time they might discover something."

The manager's lips tightened into a thin line, and she glared at Carolyn. Then she said, "All right, let her look over the hotel if she wants. But the police didn't find anything, and she won't either. If you ask me, everyone's in a stew over nothing. *I* don't hear noises. *I* don't see shadows."

"Thank you, Mrs. Zemanek." Carolyn turned to me. "Shall we start with the basement and work up to the roof?"

"That's fine with me."

Mary Zemanek said, "You can't go out on the roof. Door's always locked. The owner doesn't like—"

"Perhaps you'll let us have the key." Carolyn held out her hand.

The manager looked at it, then shrugged and took a key off a ring that was hooked to the belt loop of her plain black dress. "If you get hurt, it's not my fault."

"Don't worry," Carolyn said, pocketing the key. "We'll be careful." She started for a fire door in the wall opposite the desk.

Mary Zemanek came out of her apartment and walked stiffly over to the desk, one hand pressed to the small of her back. She removed a couple of advertising circulars that had been left there, then contemplated the Christmas tree. "I should take that down. It's a fire hazard. Those packages are an invitation to thieves."

Carolyn turned, looking as if she was about to make a reference to Ebenezer Scrooge.

"I won't, though," Mrs. Zemanek went on. "Someone would only put another in its place." She paused, still studying the tree, then added wistfully, "Besides, it looks nice. And the owner probably won't show up again until after the New Year." Slowly she walked back to her apartment.

Carolyn and I pushed through the fire door and went down a hall, past three other apartments, to a second door. "She's not as tough as she tries to act," I said.

"Mary? No. She's as frightened by these goings-on as anyone here, but she feels she has to set a brave example. Her way of doing that is to pretend nothing's happening."

Carolyn held open the second fire door and I stepped onto a stairway landing.

The walls were the same dull green as in the hallway, and the steps were gray concrete with worn metal tread. A bare bulb gleamed in a ceramic wall fixture. The door shut behind us with a sigh from its pneumatic mechanism.

"This is the stairwell where the kids saw the shadows." Carolyn's voice bounced hollowly off the walls that enclosed us.

"Which way first?" I asked. "Up or down?"

"Down, I think." She reached for a switch next to the door and a light flashed on below. I started down there, clutching the cold metal railing, my footsteps echoing.

"What about the owner?" I asked. "Mrs. Zemanek's attitude toward him seems to stop just short of reverence."

"I think it's more like the fear of God. His name is Roy LaFond, and he's by no means your typical slum landlord."

"I've heard the name somewhere."

"LaFond is a big Marin County real estate developer. He did that Bay Shores condominium project in Tiburon."

"That's why it sounds familiar. How'd he end up owning a place like this?"

"Mrs. Zemanek says he took it as part of a larger deal about a year ago. You know—the sort of thing where the former owner wanted to unload it and gave LaFond a lower price on some property he really wanted in exchange for taking the Globe off his hands. Anyway, LaFond seems genuinely horrified to possess a Tenderloin hotel full of Vietnamese and other social misfits."

We reached the bottom of the stairway and stopped. To our right was a bank of plywood storage lockers, most of them secured with padlocks. Straight ahead was the gray metal hulk of a furnace. And to one side of the furnace a clumsy old-fashioned boiler stood on absurd spindly legs. It reminded me of a big white cow that had grown too fat for her underpinnings.

"Quiet down here, isn't it?" I said. "The furnace isn't on.

15

Is one of the disputes you mentioned over heat?" Heat was a major problem in the Tenderloin. A few years ago the morning paper had run a series of articles exposing the "heat cheats," landlords whose skimping forced tenants— the majority of whom were elderly and needed more warmth than most people to stay healthy—to wear coats at all hours and sleep in several layers of clothing. As a result, the city inspectors had swept the hotels, demanding proof that they were being heated the legally requisite eleven hours per day. Owners had been fined, some had been jailed, and compliance had been forced. But now heat was a dead issue, having been milked by the media for all it was worth, and many hotels had become cold once again.

"No," Carolyn said. "Roy LaFond stays strictly within the letter of the law."

"I noticed the hotel is better maintained than most."

"No thanks to the owner. The Vietnamese are a tidy people; they can't abide dirt, and they don't wait for someone else to clean up after them. This place was a pigsty when we moved the first family in over two years ago. You'd never know that now."

I nodded and looked around the basement. It was as tidy as the upstairs halls, and there didn't seem to be anyplace a person could hide. The storage lockers were flush against the walls. A small person might be able to squeeze behind the furnace, but that was the first place any searcher would look. And the walls were all solid cinderblock; there were no niches, vents, or other recesses. I supposed someone could have climbed up on the overhead heat ducting, but it didn't look like it would support much more than a child's weight.

I went over to the boiler and touched its curving side; it was warm. "Plenty of hot water."

"Yes."

"So what *were* the disputes over, then?"

"LaFond stays too much within the law. He's deathly afraid of being cited or having something happen that will force his insurance rates up. He's always issuing directives

16

through Mary Zemanek—they're perfectly legal but they make life here very rough."

"Such as?"

"Well, for one thing, the children are not allowed to play in the halls or the lobby. That creates a difficult situation for tenants with active youngsters. The stairs are officially off limits to them too. And that makes things damned near impossible when the elevator's not working." Anger had come into Carolyn's voice; even in the dim light I could see that her face was flushed.

"I take it the rules aren't always observed, since Billy and Jenny saw the shadows in the stairwell."

"Of course they're not! They're ridiculous. And this thing about the roof being locked—there's a lot of room up there, and high barriers so no one could possibly fall. It would be an ideal place for the children to play, plus the people could grow vegetables in containers. The tenants got together and petitioned LaFond to let them use it. His reply? A flat 'no,' delivered through Mary Zemanek."

"What about the Christmas tree? Would he really demand it be removed, as Mrs. Zemanek hinted?"

"He'd probably throw it in the trash himself—plus rip the decorations off the fire escape. To the Roy LaFonds of the world, the Vangs and the others here simply aren't people with normal human needs. They're rent-paying units. And if the laws didn't prevent it, you can bet their rents would have tripled in the last year."

I watched Carolyn, surprised at her vehemence. I'd seen her under some of the worst of circumstances, and she'd always been rational and controlled. Too controlled, perhaps. I was glad to glimpse this fire under her cool exterior.

In the silence, she began shaking her head ruefully. "Forgive me, but I get so angry. In my work I see too many people like the Vangs, who have been through so much. They've fled their homeland, lost everything, and yet they go on striving. To me, they're heroic people; to Roy La-Fond, who's had everything handed him all his life, they're dirt."

17

I thought about that, then said cautiously, "Do you really know that Roy LaFond has had it so easy?"

She shrugged and turned away. "I know the type. And now we'd better take a look at the rest of the stairwell and the roof. I assume you've seen all you want to down here."

"I will have in a minute." I went over to the storage lockers and began opening those that weren't secured by padlocks. The first two were empty; the third contained a cardboard roach trap and a box of miscellaneous nails and screws; the fourth was crammed with some sort of dark material. I pulled it out and spread it on the floor.

It was a sheet, an old, tattered one, in an ugly olive green. There were two neatly cut holes near its center. I picked it up and held the holes to my eyes.

"What's that?" Carolyn said.

"Looks like your basic Halloween ghost costume."

"In dark green? I doubt it. Besides, what's it doing down here?"

"Maybe some former tenant forgot it. Or . . ." I looked thoughtfully at the sheet.

Carolyn waited.

"You know," I said, "this could be what the prankster uses to make those shadows on the stairwell walls. A person could look very scary in shadow if he was wearing this and waving the material around."

"I guess so. But if that's the case, why didn't Mrs. Zemanek or Duc and his friends find it when they investigated down here?"

"If you recall, they were looking for a person who was making noise in this room, not the creature in the stairwell. Besides, even if they'd seen this, to them it probably would have been just an old sheet."

She looked dubious, but didn't say anything.

I bundled the sheet up and stuffed it under my arm. "I'll bring it along tonight and ask if anyone knows who it belongs to. If no one recognizes it, this could be our first concrete evidence that someone really is trying to frighten these people." Then I motioned at the stairs. "Let's see if we can find anything else on the roof."

We went up seven flights, and Carolyn unlocked the door to the roof. As she had said, there were high concrete parapets around the periphery, topped by a tall chain-link barrier. It might not be a good place for children to play unsupervised, but under the eye of a vigilant adult, no harm could possibly come to them. And there was ample room for a container garden.

I made a thorough search, finding nothing, then crossed to the west side and looked out over the rooftops. I was beginning to feel some of the same anger Carolyn had expressed, and as if she sensed that, she came up beside me and said, "You know, sometimes I feel so helpless. There's so much these people—my people—need and so little I can do for them. The Center doesn't have the staff or the money. Every year we think we won't get re-funded, and there's always a two-month gap when we exist on credit and do without salary waiting to hear what the government agencies and private foundations will dole out to us. And then I see someone like Roy LaFond, who could help if he wanted to . . ."

"I think I understand."

She studied my face for a moment, then nodded decisively. "Yes, I guess you do."

I looked back out over San Francisco, seeing the squalid roofs of the Tenderloin and, beyond them, the curves of the hills and the skyscrapers where the rich people lived. More and more lately it seemed to me that there was so much unnecessary waste in the world, waste of our precious resources—be they forests or endangered species of animals. Or people. And most of it stemmed from the same reason that made Roy LaFond keep this roof locked and off limits. Simple cowardice—the inability to take a personal risk or make a stand for what one knew was right— was dressed up as looking out for Number One, as watching out for that old bottom line.

Maybe, I thought, I didn't belong in this world of the nineteen-eighties, where things counted more than people. Maybe I was too much a child of the sixties, a throwback to a time when many of us had tried to care about one another. But I couldn't change that; I'd just have to muddle along, doing what I could in my own small way. And one thing I could do was try to make matters better for these people—here in the Globe Hotel, in San Francisco's Tenderloin, on this wintry day in the eighties.

— 3 —

Carolyn had to get back to her office, so I said I'd check in with her later. We parted on the sidewalk in front of the hotel, and I watched her hurry off toward Market Street, her shiny hair bouncing as she made her way among the slower-moving pedestrians. A tall black man—wearing only jeans and an open leather vest in spite of the December chill—stopped to stare at her with obvious pleasure. Carolyn brushed by him, her pace not faltering. He turned, made a move to follow her, then shrugged and continued on his way.

When I was sure the man wasn't going to change his mind and go after her, I went to my car and locked the olive-green sheet in the trunk. Then I looked up Eddy Street toward the corner. There was a grocery store, Tran's Fine Foods, and I could see a pay phone just inside its door. I went up there, skirting three old women in black who looked as if they'd just come from Mass and a strolling blond girl in hotpants, an early riser for San Francisco's hooking community. When I got to the phone I discovered I had no change, but the wizened Oriental man behind the grocery counter willingly broke a dollar for me. I called Marin County information, got Roy LaFond's office number in San Rafael, and called to make an appointment. Monday was his busy day, his secretary said, but he could make time for me at two o'clock.

Hanging up the receiver, I looked at my watch. Five past eleven. Three hours to kill, and I might as well spend most of it in the neighborhood. I turned back to the counter and watched the old man ring up the sale of a pack of cigarettes. A transistor radio on a shelf behind him was blaring rock-and-roll, and when the song ended, the announcer came on with the call letters: KSUN, the Light of the Bay. It was the station where my friend Don worked—a raucous, rowdy, and thoroughly ear-splitting frequency on the dial. I wondered why the old man wanted to endanger his eardrums with it.

When the customer had left, I went up to the counter and said, "Excuse me, are you the owner?"

"Yes, ma'am. Hung Tran, at your service. What may I do for you?" His accent was heavy, but his pronunciation was clear and precise.

"My name is Sharon McCone, Mr. Tran. I'm a private detective, working for some of the people who live at the Globe Apartment Hotel."

He nodded, displaying no surprise at my occupation.

"Do you know any of the Globe's residents?" I asked.

"Yes, I do. This is the nearest market. Many of them shop here."

I looked around. While the store was stocked with the standard items you find in any city grocery, there were also distinctly Oriental foodstuffs—big sacks of rice, tins of soy sauce, *bok choy* in the produce section. "Then perhaps," I said, "you know of the frightening things that have been happening at the Globe?"

"Yes, a number of the people have spoken of them to me. This is what they have hired you to find out about?"

"Yes."

"I hope you will be able to help them." His eyes, behind gold-rimmed spectacles, were polite but emotionless.

"I hope so too. Mr. Tran, who do you think is responsible for frightening those people?"

Now he looked surprised. "I? I have no opinion."

"But surely you must hear things. People talk. In your

21

position you must know a great deal about what goes on in the neighborhood."

He laced his waxy-looking hands together across the front of his gray smock. "People talk, yes. But what they say often makes no sense."

"Still, it would help me to know what they are saying."

His eyes strayed toward the door. The girl in hotpants stood there, arranging her fall of elaborately teased blond hair with the aid of her reflection in the plate glass. Mr. Tran's lips curled, then he looked back at me. "They say many things. Some think it is the owner of the building, who seeks to remove the people so he can rent the apartments at a higher rate."

"Do you believe that?"

"I have seen this owner. He is not one to hide in basements."

"What else?"

"They say it is the young men, the *bui doi.*"

"*Bui doi?*"

"In my language, it means 'the dust of life.' You would call them gangs."

"Street gangs, juvenile delinquents?"

"That is what outsiders say. They do not understand that in our culture we do not have gangs like those of your black or Chinese or Chicano citizens. If this is the work of the *bui doi,* it is far more serious than teenagers. But I do not see what interest they would have in that hotel."

I made a mental note to call a man I knew on the police department's Gang Task Force and find out about the so-called dust of life.

"What else do the people say?" I asked.

"That this is the work of a sick person. There are many in the neighborhood." Again Mr. Tran's eyes went to the door, but the hooker had moved away.

"Any one person in particular?"

"They mention the prostitutes and their pimps, but of course that is nonsense. Those ones care only about money. They talk of Brother Harry, the street preacher."

"The man with the sandwich boards?"

22

"Yes. He claims to be a man of God, but he is full of hate."

"How so?"

"His message is one of vengeance. Listen to him. You will understand."

"I'll do that. Is there anyone else in particular?"

The old man spread his hands. "In this neighborhood we have derelicts and bag ladies, and criminals who prey on them. We have many homeless persons. There are people who act strangely—who shout or glare at others on the street. There are those who use drugs and would kill for them. Who is to say which one might be responsible?"

Suddenly my job loomed large—and dangerous. I said, "But there's no one in particular whom people talk about?"

"They speak of one or another from time to time, especially if he or she has had a recent outburst of violence. But no one more than the others."

"I see." I paused, then picked up a Hershey bar from a display on the counter and dug in my bag for money.

Hung Tran held up a waxy hand. "Please, accept it with my thanks."

"But it's I who should be thanking you for the information you've given me."

"No, you are helping my people. It is the least I can do."

Touched, I mumbled my thanks and put the candy bar in my pocket. "May I come to see you again, if I have more questions?"

"Certainly." His nod was almost a bow.

The street preacher, Brother Harry, was still in front of the Sensuous Showcase Theatre. He stood on a small square of blue carpet that he had spread on the sidewalk to the right of the marquee, waving his arms and exhorting all to come back to God. The signboards he wore said PRAY TO JESUS in front. One particularly vigorous gesture turned him partially around and I made out the words HE WILL ANSWER on the rear.

In spite of his vociferous message, Brother Harry wasn't

23

drawing much of an audience. A few pedestrians eyed him with wary curiosity, but most ignored him, hurrying past with their gaze straight ahead or on the ground. Still others went up to the theatre's glassed-in ticket booth, paid their money to the heavily made-up clerk, and went inside. Undaunted, Harry preached on.

"He is waiting, brothers and sisters. He is waiting for you to come back to Him. His love is eternal, all-forgiving. But time passes quickly. And the end of the world approaches. There will be fire, flood, and pestilence. Only those who have come back to God, through Jesus Christ our Savior, will survive!

"Blood will run in the streets! Your children will scream in agony! Your own flesh will burn! The sinner will writhe in torment! None will be spared! Thus will be the punishment of he who does not accept God!

"Return, sinner! Return or else . . ."

Beside me, a man's voice spoke. It said, "'They must to keep their certainty accuse . . . all that are different of a base intent.'"

I started and turned. The man who stood there was probably in his fifties, with longish gray hair and a thick beard and mustache. His nose was elfin, his cheeks rosy, and the full mouth that was visible through the surrounding hair curved up in delight. He wore baggy khaki pants and a worn brown corduroy jacket—standard Tenderloin attire.

Deciding he was harmless, I asked, "What did you say?"

Patiently he repeated, "'They must to keep their certainty accuse . . . all that are different of a base intent.'" The rhythm in which he spoke indicated he was probably quoting poetry. More loudly, he added, "'Pull down established honor; hawk for news . . . whatever their loose phantasy invent.'"

Brother Harry stopped preaching and looked over at us, his eyes becoming slits in his fleshy, weather-roughened face.

The other man continued reciting, louder and louder. I backed off.

24

Harry balled his fists and started toward the man, his signboards flopping clumsily. "You get out of here, you poetry-mouthing wimp! Get off my corner!"

"'Truth flourishes where the student's lamp has shone, and there alone—'"

Harry grabbed the man by the collar of his jacket and began shaking him. He was a head taller and looked more vigorous, in spite of the cumbersome sandwich boards. I stepped further back as Harry shouted, "This is my corner! Off!"

Surprisingly, the other man's eyes were sparkling, and his mouth still curved up in a smile. A crowd had begun to gather behind me, and he turned his head and said, "William Butler Yeats. 'The Leaders of the Crowd.' Now, that was a man who knew about God."

Harry's face grew red and he continued to shake the man, sandwich boards heaving violently. The other man just smiled, his head bobbing this way and that. Harry's face grew redder, both from fury and exertion. Just when it looked as if he might really hurt the man, someone stepped up behind him and grabbed his arm above the elbow.

"Let go of him, Harry," the newcomer said.

Harry whirled, still clutching the poetry quoter. "Get your goddamn mitts off me, Otis."

"I said, let go."

Harry looked at the poetry quoter and gave him one last shake, then let go reluctantly, like a puppy relinquishing a bone. The man stumbled back a few feet, still smiling, and stuck his hands in his jacket pockets. He stood there, rocking back and forth from heels to toes.

I looked at the man who had broken up the confrontation. He was slender, with fine light brown hair, wearing jeans, a colorful red cowboy shirt, and elaborately tooled leather boots with two-inch heels. Letting go of the street preacher's arm, he glanced at the bearded man and said, "Beat it, Jimmy. Go recite your poetry someplace else."

The man called Jimmy just grinned at him.

"Get!"

With a shrug, Jimmy ambled off across the street. Once he reached the other curb, he stopped and stood there, then thumbed his nose.

The cowboy sighed and turned back to the street preacher. "Why do you let him get to you, Harry? You know Jimmy likes to see you all riled up."

Harry glared over at Jimmy, a muscle jumping in his jaw. "Otis, the son-of-a-bitch keeps messing up my preaching. I ought to kill him, him and his William Butler Yeats."

"Well, Harry, the way I hear it, Yeats has been dead for years. And killing Jimmy wouldn't be good P.R." The cowboy named Otis waved emphatically for Jimmy to go away. Jimmy thumbed his nose again.

"There—you see, Otis?" Harry said. "He's gonna stand there and mess up my act. How am I supposed to get through to these sinners when he's doing that?"

"I guess you won't, right now. So why don't you take a break? He'll get bored if you leave and go someplace else."

"But I was really warming up."

"Take a break, Harry."

Anger flashed across the street preacher's fleshy face, and then he turned and lumbered back to his square of carpet. He bent down clumsily, rolled the carpet up, and stood, tucking it under his sandwich boards. "Sometimes I think you're on his side, Otis," he said.

Otis sighed again. "That's your trouble, Harry. You don't understand people. I'm on *my* side. Mine. Nobody else's." Then he turned and strode off into the Sensuous Showcase Theatre.

Harry said, "Huh. The hell I don't understand people." He gave Jimmy one last glare and headed around the corner onto Jones Street.

I looked over at the bearded man and saw his face fall. He shoved his fists into his pockets, kicked at the curb a time or two, and then shuffled off, his head bent despondently. The small crowd that had gathered began to disperse.

I glanced at the marquee of the theatre. Something

26

called *Rajah* was playing on a triple bill with *A Mother's Love* and *The Reluctant Couple*. I looked at my watch, decided I had time, and followed the man named Otis.

— 4 —

No one was in the ticket booth when I went up to it, so I just walked into the lobby of the theatre. The man called Otis stood to one side of the doors talking with the jowly, heavily made-up woman who had been collecting admission fees. The lobby was small, draped in red and black velvet and bathed in what was probably supposed to be sensuous crimson light. All the light did, however, was emphasize the worn spots on the velvet hangings and carpet. Beyond the doors to the main part of the theatre I could hear the mutterings of a sound track.

When I came in, Otis broke off his conversation with the woman, frowning. "Better get back out there, Ruth. They're wandering in without paying."

As he spoke, I realized who he must be: Otis Knox, one of the kingpins of San Francisco's porn industry. Knox owned this theatre, as well as two others, plus was involved in film production and distribution. He was one of a handful of operators—along with the famous Mitchell Brothers—who claimed to be legitimate entrepreneurs selling a necessary and desirable product. In a recent newspaper interview, Knox had been photographed astride a horse at his ranch in an undisclosed Marin County location. The article quoted him as saying he was just a country boy trying to make an honest buck. Why he was always being hassled by the D.A.'s office was something he couldn't understand. He'd claimed to be providing employment for a lot of people—including women who might otherwise be out on the streets. One quote that remained in my mind was: "And I keep a lot of lawyers busy. That's all the D.A.'s harassment does—puts money in the pockets of my lawyers, who don't need it anyway."

Now Knox came toward me, barring further entrance. Up close I could see he was older than he'd looked on the street—in his late forties—and that his light brown hair was blow-dried backwards in an attempt to disguise a spreading bald spot.

"You want to see the movie, you have to pay," he said, glancing at the woman, who was disappearing through a door to the ticket booth. "Go back outside, she'll be glad to take your money."

"It's not the film I'm interested in, Mr. Knox," I said. "I'd like to talk with you."

"If you're a reporter, I don't give interviews on short notice. Call and set up an appointment."

"I'm not a reporter." I took out the photostat of my license and handed it to him.

He squinted at it, holding it up in the dim light. Then his lean face twisted in annoyance. "Aw, Christ! Now it's some unofficial beef. Who hired you?"

"No one who has any interest in you or your business. I saw the scene you broke up on the street between Brother Harry and the man you called Jimmy. I'd like to talk to you about them."

His annoyance turned to perplexity and he handed the photostat back to me. "You want to talk about those bums? Why?"

A couple who were easily identifiable as tourists—she carried an enormous vinyl handbag, he had a camera slung over one shoulder—came in, the woman hanging back in obvious reluctance. I said, "Is there someplace better to talk?"

Knox shrugged, then turned and headed for a door marked OFFICE. "Okay, I've got a few minutes and nothing better to do."

The office was a small cubicle jammed with the kind of

28

junk some people call collector's items. The walls were covered with signs—street signs, Yield signs, Stop signs, Men Working signs. Shelves held old beer cans, disconnected limbs of mannequins, wooden cigar boxes, a gumball machine minus the candy, Coca-Cola glasses, a mason jar full of marbles, a stack of Uncle Scrooge comic books, miscellaneous bottles, and a decoy duck. From the ceiling hung a fishnet full of glass bobbers, corks, and seashells. There was a metal desk covered with papers and two chairs in front of it—one of which held a saddle. Knox waved me toward the other chair and went around the desk. He fumbled through the papers, came up with cigarettes and matches, lit one, and put the match in an ashtray shaped like a foot.

I sat down and looked up at the fishnet. A crutch rested incongruously among the nautical items.

Knox was watching me. "You like my stuff?" He flopped into his desk chair, gesturing around us.

"It's . . . interesting."

"Yeah. A hobby of mine, collecting."

"I see."

"I've got even more at home. Bigger stuff. Jukeboxes. An old Coke machine. McDonald's Golden Arches. Babe the Blue Ox."

"What?"

"Babe the Blue Ox. A statue. Thirteen feet high. I got him when they tore down the Paul Bunyan Drive-in in Corvallis, Oregon."

"Good Lord."

Abruptly Knox's manner changed. He leaned forward on the desk and looked at me intently. "Now what's this about Brother Harry and Jimmy?"

I explained about the problems at the Globe Hotel and the suspicions that were circulating through the neighborhood. Knox listened carefully, squinting at me through a haze of smoke. When I finished, he said, "I don't know, honey. Both of those boys are as crazy as loons, but to frighten a bunch of slopes . . ."

29

Inwardly I winced at the cruel term, which had come home from Vietnam with the American military.

"I don't know," Knox repeated. "Harry's just a lunatic, has some half-cocked ideas about God. And Jimmy's a poor homeless bastard who's been run from pillar to post. It doesn't seem likely either of them—"

"Tell me about them."

He shifted in his chair, stuck one booted foot up on the corner of his desk, and leaned his head back. "Well, Harry's been around for years. Mostly preaches on this corner; I guess he thinks it's some kind of antidote for my films."

"Does he live in the neighborhood?"

"Yeah, he's got a room in a flophouse over on Turk Street. He's here rain or shine, hollering about salvation. Sometimes I chase him off, just for form's sake, but usually I let him rant."

"What's his last name?"

Knox paused. "Woods, I think. But I wouldn't swear to it."

"Do you know how he feels about the Vietnamese who have been moving into the area?"

"We've never discussed it. Probably the same as he feels about everybody else—that they're sinners who've got to be brought to God."

"What about Harry's background? Has he ever said where he came from?"

"No. He's been around here as long as I have, maybe fifteen years."

"And you don't know how he got the way he is?"

Knox shrugged. "How do any of us get crazy?"

It was a good question. "What about the man you called Jimmy? Who's he?"

"Jimmy Milligan. Sad case. He's educated—you can tell that, the way he recites that poetry. Yeats. Always Yeats, nothing else. But his moods go up and down fast, without much warning."

I'd noticed that a little while ago. "Is he violent?"

30

Knox smiled, a little surprised. "Jimmy? Hell, no. Just real happy or real sad. One minute he'll be grinning like an idiot—like he was out there at Harry—next he's looking like he might cry. Does cry, sometimes. Stands there on the street and bawls."

"You said something about him being homeless."

"Yeah. Jimmy's one of these proud people—won't take welfare or sleep at the Salvation Army or Glide Memorial. He sets up places to live in abandoned buildings, old newspaper kiosks, in the holes at construction sites. You name it, Jimmy's tried it. Makes the places pretty nice—I remember one time he even hung curtains in this big wooden crate somebody left in an alley. But the cops always come along and roust him. The cops or the people who own the property or the housing authority. Happens every time."

"Where does Jimmy live now?"

Knox shrugged. "Who knows? It's been a couple of months since he was chased off that lot where the Rendezvous Bar burned down over on Ellis Street."

"Why does Jimmy taunt Brother Harry?"

"Why would anybody taunt Harry? He's got no sense of humor and a real short fuse. It's kind of fun to watch him explode."

Some people, I reflected, had an odd idea of fun. "Let me ask you this, Mr. Knox," I said. "Do you have any idea of who might be trying to frighten the people at the Globe?"

He hesitated, as if he were trying to decide whether to say something or not. I waited. Finally he took his foot off the desk and said, "I've got no ideas. None at all. I'm just a country boy, trying to make a living as best I can. I'll tell you—I should have been a cowhand. I come into the city every day, do my bit, but by nightfall, I'm back on the ranch with my horses."

"I see." It was the same folksy line he'd trotted out for the newspaper reporter. "But you're here in the neighborhood every day. Don't you hear things—"

"Honey, I got three theatres to run. This is my headquar-

31

ters, but I'm out half the time at the other two. And there's the production company, and the hassles with the D.A., and the lawyers. . . . I tell you, I'm up to my ears in work. I got no time to entertain ideas about who's trying to scare a bunch of slopes."

I merely watched him. After a moment, he added, "Yeah, honey, I'm real busy. The business is growing; we're making a big move."

"Oh?"

"Yeah. You know the old Crystal Palace Theatre over on Market Street?"

I nodded.

"I bought it last week. Going to consolidate operations, give this town the biggest and best adult entertainment center ever."

The Crystal Palace Theatre was one of the ornate relics left over from the early part of the century. It had been standing empty and unused for years now. Several preservationist groups had attempted to have historical landmark status approved for it, but so far had been unsuccessful. I frowned, wondering if their membership knew of Otis Knox's plans for the structure.

Knox didn't seem to notice my displeasure. He lit another cigarette and leaned back in his chair again, his eyes dreamy through the smoke. "It's some place, that theatre. Downright shabby now, but what a history it's got. You know anything about it?"

"No, but—"

"The first Crystal Palace was built in the 1860s. They called those times the 'Sensation Era'—and I guess it sure was. Variety shows. Burlesques. Minstrels. Performers like Lotta Crabtree, Eddie Foy, Lola Montez. You heard of them?"

I nodded, surprised at his interest in the history of his purchase.

"Yeah, those were some days," Knox went on. "Of course, the original theatre was destroyed in the oh-six 'quake and fire. Only one in the city—I forget which—survived. But they rebuilt, and then you had vaudeville and all that. They say the owners of the Crystal Palace even built a speakeasy under Market Street during Prohibition. Tunneled right out there under the streetcar tracks, and all the fancy ladies and gentlemen would sit and tipple while the cars rumbled along over their heads."

"Have you seen the speakeasy?"

"Nope. They say the tunnel was closed off in the thirties. *I* say the story's pure legend. Otherwise they'd have found it when they excavated for BART and the Muni Metro. But if it existed—what couldn't I do with it! Anyway, the theatre fell on hard times after the movies came in. For a while in the seventies some promoter tried to convert it for rock concerts, but they didn't go over. Kids who go to things like that need space, don't want to be told to stay in their seats. So the place has been standing empty for years."

"And now it's going to become a porn palace."

I'd expected that to annoy him, but he merely shrugged. "I don't pretend to be any better than I am. It's a business, that's all."

At that moment the door opened behind me. I glanced back and saw a gangly youth with limp black hair standing there. "Mr. Knox," he said, "there's something wrong with the projector."

"Christ, Arnie, now what?"

The youth gestured vaguely; he looked half stoned. "I don't know. Can you come?"

"In a minute." Knox stood up. The projectionist went out and Knox smiled at me, spreading his arms in a placating gesture. "Look," he said, "I'm not the bad guy everybody thinks I am. You ought to get to know me better. You should come over to Nicasio sometime—play the jukeboxes, a little pinball. I'll even introduce you to Babe the Blue Ox."

Unwilling to offend him in case I needed additional information later on, I said, "You know, Mr. Knox, maybe someday I'll take you up on that offer. Babe sounds like quite a guy."

*　　*　　*

33

Neither Brother Harry nor Jimmy Milligan was in sight when I emerged from the theatre, and the people on the street were the usual ragtag assortment. Once again I checked my watch, and since I still had time before I had to leave for San Rafael, I went back to the Globe Hotel in hopes of talking with Sallie Hyde.

I didn't have to look far for her. She stood in the center of the lobby, clutching one of the branches from the Christmas tree. Mary Zemanek was in the doorway to her apartment, and two Vietnamese children—preschoolers—peeked out from behind the desk.

The little plastic tree had been ripped apart, branches and smashed ornaments strewn all over the floor. The packages looked as if they had been stomped on. Both of the women and the children were very still.

I said, "What's happened here?"

Sallie turned slowly. Her eyes were full of shock and grief. "Someone . . ." She motioned feebly with the tree branch.

Mary Zemanek cleared her throat. "It's what comes of setting out a temptation in the middle of a neighborhood like this." But under the stern words, I could tell she was shaken too.

"When did this happen?" I asked.

Sallie shook her head.

"It had to be within the last hour," Mary said. "Since you and that woman from the Refugee Center were here." She paused, then said to Sallie, "I trust you'll see this is cleaned up?"

The fat woman merely nodded. Mary went back into her apartment. I looked for the children, but they had disappeared.

"You don't suppose she. . . ?" I motioned toward Mary's door.

"No." Sallie sighed heavily and began gathering the torn branches. "Mary liked the tree as much as any of us; she just didn't want to be responsible."

I knelt and began helping her. "Who, then?"

"I don't know."

"The same person who's been trying to scare all of you?"

"Maybe."

"I found something this morning, in the basement. An old olive-green sheet with eyeholes cut in it. Someone could have worn it to make those shadows in the stairwell."

Sallie continued picking up fragments of ornaments.

"Have you ever seen anyone with that sheet?"

She paused, then shook her head. "No."

I swept some small fragments of red glass together, then looked for a receptacle to put them in. "Will you get a new tree?"

"I don't know." She straightened up and set the debris she'd gathered on the reception desk. "I loaned this tree to the hotel; it seemed so much better to share it than to keep it in my room. But now I wish I hadn't. I liked the tree. I've had it for years. Ever since . . . ever since I came to the hotel. Who would do such a thing?" Her words were tinged with resignation that verged on despair.

I pushed the last of the ornament fragments together, being careful not to cut myself. "That's what I'm going to find out."

Sallie went around the desk and dragged out a wastebasket. She dropped the wreckage that sat on the desk into it, then helped me dispose of the pieces of glass. "The city's changing," she said as she stood up. "This never would have happened before."

"Before what?"

"Oh, nothing in particular. I mean, years ago. The city's so different now. There's so much anger in people. The other day I was in the crosswalk in front of Magnin's, by the Square, where my flower stand is. Walking with the light. This guy in a sports car—nice-looking, well-dressed guy, what we used to think of as a gentleman—turns the corner, almost hits me. I jump back as he screeches on the brakes, and you know what he says to me? 'Fuck you, lady.'" She finished dumping the remains of the gift packages into the basket, then placed it out of sight behind the desk.

35

"'Fuck you, lady,'" she repeated wearily. "And that, from what we used to call a gentleman."

I could see she was in no mood to answer the kind of questions I wanted to ask her, so I said, "Will you be home tonight, Sallie?"

"Tonight? I'm always home at night. Don't like to be on the streets after dark."

"I'll stop by and see you then."

"Sure. Stop by any time." The fat woman made her way to the elevator, looking years older than she had when I'd met her that morning.

— 5 —

Roy LaFond's office was located north of downtown San Rafael, in a new area of industrial parks. I drove up there on Route 101, past rolling hills that were newly green from the early winter rains.

Marin County presented a marked change from the Tenderloin. Expensive homes clung to the hillsides, commanding sweeping vistas of Mount Tamalpais and Richardson Bay. The marinas were choked with sailboats, chic shopping centers lined the freeway, and luxury cars roared by me as I nursed my ancient MG up the steep grades. This was affluent land—notorious for the somewhat hackneyed hot tub and peacock feather—the spiritual capital of the Me Generation. But Marin also had pockets of poverty; a soup kitchen in San Rafael was dispensing more free meals than ever before, and requests from charities for donations of clothing and household goods for the needy were well publicized. Like the Tenderloin, Marin had its problems, but they were easier to ignore amidst all this natural beauty.

I exited from 101 at Freitas Parkway and took the curving off ramp over the freeway to Northgate Drive. It wound past a large shopping center, crowded with people seeking holiday gifts. LaFond's building was a standard redwood-and-glass office complex on the right-hand side, just beyond Sears. I parked in front, went inside, and wandered the corridors for a few minutes before I found his suite.

The reception area was furnished with good antiques and a central table displaying a relief map of the Bay Shores condominium project in Tiburon. No one was behind the desk. I waited, then cleared my throat loudly, and finally a young woman appeared in a doorway at the rear, her arms full of collated papers. Her hair straggled loose from a barrette at the nape of her neck and, despite the relative serenity of the offices, she appeared harried. "Oh," she said, "you must be Roy's two o'clock appointment."

I looked at my watch. It was two-ten. "Yes. I'm sorry I'm late."

The woman dumped the papers on the reception desk. "You may be late, but Roy's later. He just called in five minutes ago and said he's been delayed at the new job site. And he suggested you might want to meet him there, to save time."

"Where is the job site?"

"Bay Shores East, over in Alameda County near Golden Gate Fields."

I considered. It was a relatively short drive from here, over the Richmond–San Rafael Bridge, and later I could return to the city via the Bay Bridge. "All right, I'll do that."

She gave me directions and said she would call LaFond on his car phone and tell him I was on my way. I went out to my car and retraced my route to the freeway.

The approach to the bridge went past San Quentin Prison, its high walls a deceptively pleasant peach color in the afternoon sun. The bridge's span rose over the placid waters of the Bay, and then the road—its pavement roughened and scarred by the constant heavy truck traffic—cut through an industrial area and eventually joined the East-shore Freeway. LaFond's new condominium development was easy to spot, on a point of land that jutted out into the Bay near the big racetrack. Concrete pads had already been poured for the buildings, and steel girders rose sky-ward from them.

I drove through the opening in the chain-link fence around the construction site and asked a man in a hardhat where to find Mr. LaFond. He pointed at three men who were leaning on the tailgate of a pickup truck, discussing some blueprints. "He's the one with the white hair."

Leaving the car near the fence, I started toward the men. They looked around as I approached, and then the white-haired man said a few words to the others, slapped one on the shoulder, and came toward me. He was tall and slender, dressed in casual clothes that would be equally at home on a construction site or a golf course, and his face was tanned and virtually unlined. The hair, I thought, had to be prematurely white.

"Ms. McCone?" He extended his hand. "I'm Roy La-Fond. Thanks for coming over here. I would have met you at the office, but a problem came up between my architect and my structural engineer that had to be resolved right away."

"No trouble." I gestured at the steel girders. "I take it this is going to be another complex like the one you built in Tiburon."

He smiled in pleasure, laugh lines crinkling at the corners of his eyes. "You know Bay Shores, then?"

"I've seen it from a distance."

"Well, Bay Shores East will be even better. Five hundred units, two- and three-bedrooms. Pool, Jacuzzi, health spa, boat landing, full security, and—of course—the view of San Francisco across the Bay." His voice was boyish and enthusiastic, lilting at the end of phrases.

I took a good look at Roy LaFond and decided the grocer Hung Tran had been right—this was not a man to lurk in basements or frighten children in stairwells. Still, this might be a man who would hire someone to lurk . . .

". . . interested in buying one, I suppose?"

I turned my attention back to what LaFond was saying. "I'm sorry?"

"I don't suppose you'd be interested in buying one of our units?"

He seemed to be making a joke, but I sensed a seriousness beneath the words. Roy LaFond, from what I'd heard of him, had made a lot of money for someone who couldn't be more than forty, and he'd probably done so by never letting an opportunity to make a deal pass him by.

I said, "Sorry, but I doubt I could afford one." I didn't add that I wouldn't want one either. There had been a time when I'd thought I preferred sleek modern homes and furnishings. But the older I got, the more I leaned toward the traditional. My five-room cottage, built as emergency housing after the earthquake of 1906, suited me perfectly.

At that moment, a flatbed truck bearing a load of steel rumbled through the gate. LaFond put a hand on my arm and moved me out of its path, in spite of it being many yards away. Leaning down toward me, he said, "My secretary tells me you want to talk about the Globe Hotel. Are you a prospective buyer?"

I was about to explain my interest in the hotel when the driver of the truck jumped down from the cab and began hollering at a group of workers who were idling nearby. I glanced over there and said, "Could we find someplace quieter to talk?"

"Certainly. Let's go down by the jetty." Taking my arm again, as if he were afraid I might trip on the uneven ground, LaFond led me across the site to the bay shore, where a wall of natural rock rose above the water. I smiled faintly, remembering his concern about his insurance rates. He didn't let go of me until I was firmly ensconced on the jetty, then stepped back and stood before me, feet placed wide, arms folded across his chest.

"I take it the brokers sent you," he said.

"No. I'm a private investigator."

Concern flared in his eyes. "What's wrong over there?"

"There have been problems—"

"Who hired you?"

"The tenants. They—"

"There's plenty of heat and hot water. I've complied with every ordinance. And I haven't tried to raise their rents."

"I know that. But there have been—"

"They have nothing to complain about. I try to be a fair landlord."

"I'm sure you do."

Agitated, LaFond began to pace. "God knows I never wanted to own that fleabag. If it hadn't been a contingency on the deal for this land, I wouldn't have touched it. I don't know a damned thing about being landlord to a bunch of slum dwellers. And I can't sell that dump; no one will even look at it, much less make an offer. And now, what is it? Have they gotten up another petition or what?"

"Mr. LaFond—"

"I can't let them up on that roof. They don't understand the insurance—"

"Mr. LaFond!" I raised my voice, as Carolyn had earlier with Mary Zemanek. "No one wants anything from you."

The words halted his pacing. "They don't?"

"No. Why don't you sit down and I'll explain."

He hesitated, then came over and leaned against the jetty next to me. "Explain, then."

"There have been problems at the hotel. Someone seems to be trying to frighten your tenants."

"Oh, that. Mary Zemanek mentioned something about it. But it was my impression that it was more hysteria than anything else."

"Perhaps. But the Refugee Assistance Center—which settled many of the Asian tenants in the hotel—is concerned enough to want me to look into it."

"They're paying you?"

"Yes."

"So none of this will come out of my pocket?"

40

"No."

"I see." He paused, obviously pleased with that. "But why have you come to me?"

"I want to get your ideas on who might be causing these incidents."

"*My* ideas? Why should I have any?"

"Well, it *is* your building."

"I own it, yes. But I haven't even set foot in it since last August. I have a manager to oversee it; don't tell me Mary's been falling down on the job."

"I'm sure she's doing the best she can. But these incidents apparently are quite frightening."

"She didn't describe them that way."

"Probably she didn't want to alarm you. But they recur. . . . Today, for instance, someone destroyed a Christmas tree that was in the lobby."

An odd look passed over LaFond's face, and then he frowned. "I can see how that could happen. That whole neighborhood's frightening. If you ask me, it's got to be some weirdo off the street who gets his kicks out of terrorizing people."

"Did you ever consider that it might be someone with an ulterior motive?"

He squinted at me through the sunlight. "What kind of motive?"

I shrugged, letting it go temporarily. "Mr. LaFond, what do you intend to do with the hotel?"

"Sell it, if I can. It's listed. But, as I said, there haven't been any takers."

"A sale would involve the buyer taking the tenants along with the building, wouldn't it?"

"That's the way the rent control ordinance reads."

"And the new owner wouldn't be able to raise the rents?"

"No. It's a real drawback to a sale. Anyone financing that building today, given what interest rates are, would be taking on a heavy debt load. And, of course, there are repairs and maintenance. The building doesn't pay for itself

41

now, let alone with higher financing." He pushed away from the wall and began to pace again. "I'd love to unload it, or turn it into something more profitable."

"Like what?"

"Well, there's nothing I *can* do, given the neighborhood. If it were a few blocks further north, it would be a good possibility for one of those bed-and-breakfast places, or a chic, small hotel. You know the Abigail—near the main library?"

I nodded.

"Well, something like that. Spruce it up, furnish it with nice Victorian antiques, stick in a lounge, maybe a little restaurant. You'd have a real money-maker. I had a prospective buyer who was considering just that sort of thing—until he took a good look at the neighborhood."

"So effectively you're stuck with the Globe—and its tenants."

"Yes." He stopped pacing and turned to look at me, openly dismayed. "I guess I am."

"Have you ever thought of getting the tenants out? It would make the property more salable."

"Of course I've thought of it. But there's no legal way to do that."

"But if they were frightened into leaving . . ."

His eyes narrowed. "What you're saying is that I'm the one who is frightening them, to get them to vacate the premises."

I just watched him, expecting an outburst of anger.

Roy LaFond surprised me. He ran a hand through his thick white hair, obviously at a loss for words. He surprised me so much, in fact, that I couldn't think of anything to say either. I was fairly certain LaFond hadn't gotten where he was by being a nice guy, and I'd taken his boyishness for an act, much like Otis Knox's "aw, shucks, honey" performance. But LaFond actually seemed puzzled—and hurt.

We looked at each other for a minute, and then he said with wounded dignity, "I assure you, Ms. McCone, I do not sneak around that hotel growling at children in the stairwell. Nor do I create power failures, make noises in the basement, or destroy Christmas trees. I may not want that building or its tenants, but it's in my best interests to make sure they are safe and secure."

I had started to feel slightly ashamed, but when he said that about his best interests, the emotion evaporated. I said, "And you have no ideas about who might be responsible for these incidents."

"No, none at all. And now I have to get back to my engineer." He held out his arm, so he could guide me back to my car and thus avoid a potential lawsuit. When we got there, I thanked him for his time and told him I'd let him know what I found out. He merely nodded perfunctorily and walked away.

I thought about Roy LaFond and his odd reaction all the way to the city. And I particularly thought about his protestation of not growling at children in the stairwell or creating power failures; initially he'd hardly seemed aware of the incidents. It would be interesting to know how much Mary Zemanek had told him. And it would also be interesting to know where Roy LaFond had been about the time that Christmas tree had been dismembered.

— 6—

By the time I got back to the city it was close to five o'clock; there would be just enough time to go to my office at All Souls Legal Cooperative in Bernal Heights and make a few phone calls before meeting Don at my house for dinner. Since I didn't intend to be there long, I left my car in the driveway of the brown Victorian and hurried up the front steps.

Ted, the secretary, was typing industriously when I came

through the door, and he nodded at me, barely taking his eyes off the handwritten notes he was transcribing. There was no sign of his usual *New York Times* crossword puzzle—or his friendly grin. A familiar flat feeling stole over me as I went down the hall and dumped my coat and bag in my office.

To banish the feeling, I continued along the narrow corridor to my boss, Hank Zahn's, office. But the door was shut and a Do Not Disturb sign—courtesy of the Doubletree Inn in Monterey—hung on the knob. I looked at it, debated knocking anyway, then went all the way to the rear of the house to the big country kitchen. No one was there, and none of the usual unwashed coffee cups and dishes cluttered the counters. The flat feeling was fast becoming a depression.

I went over to the refrigerator and looked in. A couple of bottles of Calistoga Water, some limp celery, condiments, and a withered lime. No wine, no big pots of Hank's famous beef stew, not even the alfalfa sprouts the co-op's health food addicts favored. I shut the fridge door and leaned against it, sighing.

For several months now there had been a change in the atmosphere at All Souls. Once warm, friendly, and easygoing, it was now cold and tense. People no longer took their meals here or organized impromptu parties; several of the attorneys had moved out of the living quarters on the second floor. There were conferences behind closed doors, and I was always running across people in furtive discussions in odd places like the service porch.

I had my suspicions about what was wrong and I would have liked to talk them over with someone. But Hank, my best friend there, seemed to be hiding from everyone—me included. My other good friend, Anne-Marie Altman, the co-op's tax attorney, was one of those who had moved out, so I saw less of her than before, and when I did we kept off the subject of work.

I started back to my office, considered giving Anne-Marie a call, but decided against it. She had been with All

44

Souls since before I was hired and, as a full partner, was in a position to know what was going on. But she also kept very much to herself—it had taken me years to get to know her, and then only because we'd discovered a common passion for late-night horror movies. If Anne-Marie hadn't seen fit to discuss the matter with me thus far, she either didn't know very much or didn't want to talk about it. I'd just have to wait until Hank came out of his self-imposed isolation, or until there was some sort of formal explanation.

I went into my office and checked my In box for messages. There were two, one from the contractor who was remodeling the bathroom at my house, the other from Don. I tried my home number and got a busy signal; what was the workman doing on the phone when he was supposed to be hooking up the shower? Breaking the connection, I reached for my Rolodex and looked up the number for the police department's Gang Task Force. I dialed, but my contact there, Inspector Richard Loo, was off duty. I left a message asking him to call me in the morning.

Next I called the *San Francisco Chronicle* and asked for a reporter I knew, J. D. Smith. J. D. was also gone for the day. I said to the man who had answered, "Maybe you can help me. I'm trying to find out who wrote the interview you published a few months ago with Otis Knox."

"I think that was Jeff Ellis."

"Is he there?"

"Nope. He's gone too."

Another message for either J. D. or Jeff Ellis to call me when convenient.

Next I dialed Carolyn Bui. *She* was in her office. I gave her a brief rundown on what I'd been doing all day, and we agreed to meet at the Globe Hotel at ten-thirty.

Finally I called Don at KSUN. At least I could be assured of his being available; he was on the air until six. But as it was, he couldn't take the call right away because he was reading a couple of commercials. I turned up the transistor radio I keep in the office and listened to him. According to Don's enthusiastic voice, your life wouldn't be complete until you'd checked out the new selection of records and tapes at the Record Factory. And all those kids out in San Ramon had better make it to the KSUN-sponsored Christmas extravaganza at the Civic Auditorium next Friday night. Don knew it would be terrific, because he'd be there personally to give out free KSUN T-shirts to the first fifty couples . . .

Then he made some strange honking noises, told a terrible joke, laughed uproariously, and put a record on.

"Hi, babe," his voice said at the other end of the phone line.

I turned the radio off. "I swear sometimes I wonder what I'm doing with you."

"Ah, you were listening to the show."

"Briefly. I'm glad I know it's not the real you." The real Don was a quiet man, a classical pianist who hated the mediocre rock-and-roll that was the core of KSUN's format.

"Me too. Are we on for dinner?"

"Yes, but I'll have to pick something up." We discussed what we wanted to have, settled on my special burgers with lots of cheese, and said we'd meet at my house after six. Whoever arrived first would open the wine. After I hung up, I tried to call my contractor again, but the line was still busy.

That bothered me a little. The contractor was a diminutive Australian named Barry who claimed to be very good with plumbing. As far as I was concerned, his primary virtue was that he worked cheap. Up to now he had spent a great deal of time puttering around the bathroom mumbling strange things that I took to be the way they expressed frustration in Australia. It had taken a week for Barry to install the toilet—which had previously been located in an icy cubicle on the back porch—and the principles of hot and cold water pipes still eluded him. As a result, I'd been taking my showers either at the converted warehouse loft where Don lived or at the next-door neighbors'.

46

Well, I decided, I'd know what the trouble was soon enough. No use rushing home before I did the grocery shopping.

When I left the office I noticed Ted was gone, his typewriter neatly covered. The hallway was dark, the Do Not Disturb sign still hung on Hank's door, and no convivial noises or cooking smells emanated from the kitchen. In the old days, Ted would still have been there, gabbing with the attorneys as they emerged from their offices or returned from a day in court. Hank would have been throwing together one of his wonderful concoctions for dinner and taking a lot of ribbing about incipient indigestion. I probably would have been persuaded to stay around for a glass of wine—or two or three. But now all was hushed and gloomy. I wondered if anyone would even think to put up the traditional Christmas tree in the front window this year.

Brooding over this state of affairs, I went out and found a note on my car's windshield. It read: "Sharon—Please do not park in the driveway. It is for the convenience of the attorneys only." And it was signed by Gilbert Thayer, a University of Michigan graduate who had joined the co-op last year—and whom I considered to be a large part of the current problem. I crumpled the note and dropped it on the ground where I hoped he would find it, then drove to the nearby Safeway on Mission Street. After ten minutes of picking out my groceries and thirty-five standing in line, I was on my way home to check on my contractor's latest disaster.

Home was a brown-shingled cottage on Church Street, beyond where the J-line streetcar tracks stop. It was a quiet neighborhood, peopled mainly with blue-collar workers and a sprinkling of young professionals who had bought run-down houses and were fixing them up. In the ten months I'd lived there, I'd found that casual conversations over the back fence could be highly instructive; I had learned of a good place to buy linoleum from the Halls, who lived on the left side, and had been referred to Barry by the

47

Curleys, on the right. The Curleys were the ones who now let me use their shower—no doubt out of a sense of guilt.

Both sides of the narrow street were lined with cars, parked bumper to bumper, and Don's antique gold Jaguar was in my driveway. I pulled in parallel, blocking him, and looked around for Barry's truck. It wasn't in sight—a sign I wasn't sure how to interpret. I grabbed the grocery bag, hurried up the front steps, and stood on the porch, fumbling with my keys. Once inside, I tripped over my cat, Watney, who ran to greet me; I went back toward the kitchen, scolding him. Don was at the table, drinking red wine and reading the evening paper.

Don is a big man, stocky, with a graceful bearing that one normally doesn't expect in someone his size. When I came in he stood up, his mouth curving beneath his shaggy black mustache, and planted a kiss on my cheek. I put the grocery bag down on the counter and said, "Okay, where is he?"

"What a greeting." Don went back to the table and poured me a glass of wine.

Warily I took it from his outstretched hand. "If you're giving me this before I've even taken off my coat, it means trouble. Barry tried to reach me at work, but when I called back the line was busy. I take it you saw him."

"Yes. He'll be back."

I glanced suspiciously at the hallway between the kitchen and the back porch. The bathroom opened off it, and I could see a shaft of light shining through its door. "Back from where?"

"Why don't you sit down and relax?"

"Uh-oh." But I took off my coat and sat, propping my feet on one of the other chairs. "All right, where did he go?"

Don was beginning to smile again. "To borrow some surgical tools."

I didn't know what I'd been expecting, but that definitely wasn't it. "What on earth does he need surgical tools for?"

"Well, as he explained it, he spilled a box of nails, and

48

'the bloody things ran down the bloody shower drain like a wombat into a burrow.'"

I smiled faintly. "So there are nails down the shower drain. That still doesn't explain the need for surgical tools."

"Barry can't reach the nails with any of his own implements, and they're blocking the drain. So he spent the afternoon calling around and finally located an intern friend who would loan him—"

"Oh, Lord! He's going to fish the nails out of the drain with the instruments this doctor *operates* with?"

"Well, I gather he's only an intern. They probably haven't seen much service."

"Oh, Lord! Remind me to get his name and never to go to him if I have to be under the knife!"

Don and I looked at each other, and then we both started to laugh. It quickly turned into one of our shared fits, where we got started and couldn't stop until we were red-faced, teary-eyed, and weak around our midsections. As luck would have it, Barry chose to enter in the middle of it, carrying a black medical bag. We looked at the bag, exchanged glances, and lost control all over again. Barry gave us a baleful look and continued on to the bathroom. In a bit we heard delicate rattling noises as he plumbed the pipes with forceps.

I put my finger to my lips and said, "Sssh! We've hurt his feelings."

Don rolled his eyes, clasped his hand over his mouth, and tried unsuccessfully to muffle his laughter. It was several minutes before I was calm enough to get up and start making the burgers. Contritely, I made two extra, in case Barry was hungry, and cut generous slices of cheese to go on top.

— 7 —

By ten-thirty the Tenderloin had donned a tattered neon disguise. The lights of the bars and porno theatres and cheap hotels bathed the area in red and gold, pink and green, masking the worst of its squalor. But underneath the garish trappings, one could easily see the refuse and decay, and the alleys where danger waited.

I parked my car in a guarded lot Carolyn had recommended and walked toward the Globe Hotel, my senses warily alert to the activity that ebbed and flowed around me. Hard-faced women—some dressed in gaudy finery, others in rags—went about their business or stood on corners waiting for it to materialize. Shabby men, their collars turned up against the biting cold, hustled along the pavement or leaned against the buildings, panhandling. Winos clutched their paper-encased bottles as if they were last fading hopes. From the bars came blaring music and drunken laughter; from the restaurants came the odor of grease, faintly underscored by the street smells of garbage and urine.

The door of the Globe was unlocked. I hurried inside, grateful for the first rush of warm air, then stopped in surprise. On the counter where Sallie Hyde's fake Christmas tree had stood was a small Scotch pine in a red-and-green pot. It was covered with handcrafted ornaments of the kind found in specialty stores, and an ornate gold star crowned its tip. A heavy metal chain wound around the pot. I crossed the lobby and followed the chain down behind the reception desk to where it was padlocked to one of the upright supports. Someone was taking no chances.

And rightly so: live Christmas trees did not come cheap. I knew that from pricing them. Nor did the kind of ornaments this one was festooned with. Who, I wondered, had dispensed such largesse?

I went over to the door of Mary Zemanek's apartment and knocked, but received no answer. The rest of the hotel was similarly quiet, although I could hear a radio playing and a baby crying in the apartments beyond the ground-floor fire door. It was after ten-thirty, and Carolyn hadn't arrived yet, but she'd said she might be late when I'd talked to her earlier. In her absence, I decided to reinvestigate the basement; I hadn't given it a thorough going-over that morning, and it had occurred to me that I might have missed a hiding place.

I was carrying a paper sack containing the olive-green sheet I'd found down there that morning, and for a moment I debated leaving it behind the reception desk. Then I decided to keep it with me and tucked it securely under my arm as I went through the fire door. As I passed down the corridor, the baby's crying became louder. A woman's harsh voice was raised in what I was coming to recognize as the nasal syllables of Vietnamese, and then the kind of frantic music that usually accompanies TV car chases flared up. The child either stopped crying or else its wails were drowned out by the television. I shrugged, thinking that every parent has his own way of dealing with these things.

Inside the stairwell, the single bulb glowed dully, the green walls reflecting it murkily. I flicked the switch by the door and saw a shaft of light shine on the stairs that led to the basement. Standing still, I listened to the roar of the furnace below. The sheet of paper that Mrs. Vang had given me listing the frightening incidents hadn't shown times for them, just dates. But now I realized the noises in the basement would have to have been confined to those hours when the furnace wasn't in operation; otherwise, the residents couldn't possibly have heard them.

That was good, because it probably meant whoever was causing the trouble had entered the building during the daylight hours, when someone was likely to have seen him. Probably. I'd have to check the times the noises had occurred—if anyone remembered—and also the schedule for running the furnace.

I started down the stairway, my hand on the metal railing. Halfway to the landing, I heard a click, and then the furnace quit. Apparently it was on a thermostat and switched off when the area around it reached optimal temperature, whatever that was. And, unfortunately, that fact negated my new theory. Still, it would be a good idea to try to pinpoint the times of the various incidents and then canvass the neighborhood, asking if anyone had seen a stranger entering the hotel.

Now there was another faulty theory, I thought as I rounded the corner on the landing. Why was I so sure the culprit was a stranger? Perhaps it was someone who lived right here in the hotel. The residents seemed a friendly, cohesive bunch, but so had All Souls once. The trouble at the Globe could very well be internal.

The basement was quiet now, except for little pinging noises from the hot metal of the furnace. It hulked in the shadows ahead of me, the orange flicker of its pilot light visible through the grille near the floor. The flame drew my eyes downward and I saw a path of liquid that had trickled along the slightly sloping ground toward the outside wall. It hadn't been there in the morning . . .

And then I stopped, senses sharpening as they had earlier on the street. The liquid was thick and dark, and it came from the left, where the bovine boiler stood on its absurd spindly legs. Under its bulging white belly was another pair of legs—blue-jeaned, bent at the knees, feet encased in tennis shoes.

It was a man who lay there, at the beginning of that dark liquid trail.

I sucked in my breath and hurried over to him. He lay crumpled on his side, arms outflung around his head. One cheek was pressed flat on the floor, and a widening spill of blood spread around it. He was an Oriental, about Duc Vang's age or younger.

Quickly I knelt beside him and felt his neck. His flesh was warm and pliant, but I couldn't detect any pulse from the big artery. I moved my fingers around, thinking the pulse was so faint I might have missed it. Nothing. Leaning forward, I looked at the top of his head. It was caved in, with white splinters of bone showing through the scalp.

I drew back, balancing on my heels and then tipping into a sitting position. My breath came in short, shallow gasps. This had happened before, in the presence of other dead bodies, in other places. The hyperventilation brought dizziness, and I forced my head forward, slowing my breathing with a concentrated effort. This happened more and more, whenever I saw a human life tossed aside like so much garbage . . .

In a moment I straightened up. I felt very cold, and the smell of death, pungent and foully sweet, was all around me. Strange I hadn't noticed it before.

But then, the smell wasn't very strong, really. And I hadn't been expecting it. Instead I'd been looking for . . . what? Oh, yes. A hiding place.

I scanned the room around me. No one was behind the furnace or lurking at one end of the storage lockers. I searched the concrete floor, looking for a weapon. There was nothing—no wrench, no pipe, no piece of wood—that could've done the damage to this man's head.

The furnace kicked on with a loud rumble. I jerked my head toward it, then got to my feet, stumbling over the paper sack I'd been carrying. Snatching it up, I went to the stairs and glanced back at the dead man. Nothing to do for him now. Nothing but call the police.

My limbs felt cold and heavy as I climbed the stairs and went into the hall. Should I knock on one of these doors? I wondered. No, mustn't alarm the residents. The lobby— there's a pay phone.

I ran down the hall and into the lobby. Carolyn Bui stood by the desk, looking up at the Christmas tree. She turned as I came in, and her hand flew to her mouth when she saw my face.

"Sharon," she said, "what's wrong?"

I shook my head and glanced over at the pay phone in the corner. It seemed impossible to locate a coin in my bag, much less remember the number for Homicide.

53

"Sharon—"

"Give me a couple of dimes."

"But what—"

"Some dimes! Please."

Carolyn reached into her purse and extracted the coins. I took them in icy fingers and went to the phone. She followed, pressing closer to me than I would have liked. I could feel her body stiffen as I gave the facts to the Homicide inspector who caught my call.

When I hung up, I turned to face Carolyn. Her eyes glittered, unnaturally large in the dim light. "When did this happen?" she asked.

"I don't know. Not long ago. He's still warm."

"Who is he?"

"I don't know that either. A male Oriental, about Duc Vang's age. I've never seen him before."

She started for the fire door, but I caught her arm. "Don't go down there, Carolyn. Wait for the police."

"But I have to see who—"

"No, you don't. You don't want to."

She regarded me for a few seconds, then nodded and came back toward the desk with me. I let go of her arm and set the paper sack—which was beginning to annoy me—next to the tree. Then I leaned back against the ledge to wait. The ends of my hair caught on one of the tree's branches, but I didn't bother to free them. A numbness was spreading through me, a counterreaction to that last spurt of adrenaline that had enabled me to make my call.

"We should tell Mrs. Zemanek," Carolyn said after a minute.

"She's not here."

"She's always here."

"Not tonight. Not when I knocked earlier."

"Probably she was watching TV with her headphones on. She does that sometimes." Carolyn started over there.

Once more I stopped her. "Don't. She'll raise a commotion. There'll be enough confusion later. Wait for the police."

As soon as I'd spoken, two uniformed officers stepped through the street door. They asked who had called. I said I had and showed them where to go. They went down into the basement, came back. One hurried outside. The other came over to Carolyn and me. There were questions to be answered, names and addresses to be given. I felt better, having something to do.

Then they left us alone, huddled against the desk near the Christmas tree. Carolyn said, "The Vangs will be back from their restaurant soon."

"Yes."

"Who do you suppose that is in the basement?"

"I don't know."

"I should ask to see him. Maybe I can identify him."

I said nothing, tired and steeling myself for what lay ahead.

The uniformed officers returned, followed by another patrolman. Two of them went through the fire door and began knocking on the doors of the apartments off the hall. The other stood watching Carolyn and me. Soon the lab technicians would arrive, and the coroner's men . . .

I looked up at the door and then stood up straighter, staring at the tall blond plainclothesman who had just entered. It was my old boyfriend, Lieutenant Gregory Marcus. And for the first time in the more than a year and a half since we'd broken up, I was glad to see him.

— 8 —

It was after one in the morning when I let myself into the warehouse off Third Street where Don had his loft. I hurried down the echoing corridor, past a dance studio and a metal sculpture shop, and used my key in a door that was decorated with a single gold star—Don's concession to the

Christmas season. The cavernous room beyond was dark, and I flicked on overhead spotlights that illuminated a baby grand piano, a set of drums, and three walls of stereo equipment, books, and records.

Don wasn't there, but I hadn't expected him to be. He was taping one of his celebrity talk shows tonight, with a band that was in town for a holiday show at the Cow Palace. Musicians being the nocturnal creatures they are, the taping had been arranged for ten o'clock, and afterwards they would all go out someplace for drinks and creative lie-telling. I didn't expect Don until after the bars closed at two—if then.

But I hadn't wanted to go home, not after what had happened at the Globe Hotel. And I knew Don would arrive eventually. Right now it was enough just being there among his treasured possessions. Don is a person who leaves a great deal of himself in any place he inhabits, and I could almost feel his comforting presence. I dropped my coat on a pile of pillows on his big blue rug, then went over to the piano, running my fingers over the keys and striking middle C. The note echoed forlornly in the high-ceilinged space—forlorn, like I felt.

The murder victim in the basement of the hotel had turned out to be Hoa Dinh, aged sixteen, eldest son of a family on the sixth floor and Duc Vang's best friend. Hoa, Carolyn had told me, had been only ten when his family had fled Vietnam in a cargo boat with forty other people. The boat had nearly sunk and, after losing engine power, had drifted for a week on the South China Sea before help came. Hoa had then come to America by a circuitous route; had suffered fear and deprivation and uncertainty; had been shunted between two resettlement camps, where he could neither speak the language nor eat the strange, unpalatable food. In San Francisco, he had been moved in and out of three apartments, endured the rigors of English-as-a-second-language classes, and finally begun an electronics course that promised him something of a brighter future.

He had been through all that, and then at age sixteen he'd ended up bludgeoned to death in the basement of a Tenderloin hotel.

I left the piano and climbed to the large loft on the left-hand side, where the kitchen and eating area were. On the opposite side of the space was a smaller loft where Don slept under one of the skylights. He'd found the place in October after he'd been evicted from his apartment because his piano playing disturbed the neighbors, and it was the ideal situation for him. All the spaces in the converted warehouse were soundproofed, and even if they hadn't been, Don's music would not have bothered the other tenants, who came and went at odd hours, some living in the building, others merely practicing various artistic pursuits there.

After getting myself some white wine from the refrigerator, I sat down at the oak dining table. I wanted to clear the events at the Globe Hotel from my mind; I would have liked to have drunk enough to banish the images implanted there. But that wasn't going to happen. For one thing, there wasn't enough wine to get really drunk; and even if there had been, no amount of alcohol was going to help me. I'd never been able to turn off my mind—either at will or with booze or tranquilizing drugs—and I knew I was in for a bad time.

When Greg Marcus had spotted me in the lobby of the hotel over two hours earlier, he'd raised one dark-blond eyebrow and said sardonically, "We've got to stop meeting like this."

I'd smiled faintly and stood up even straighter, wanting to present a controlled, professional appearance. It seemed to me that I should be getting better at handling these things, what with all the years and all the violence. But I wasn't. I still felt sickened and I still hyperventilated, and it made me ashamed, especially when I reacted that way in front of a pro like Greg.

As he watched my face, his eyes flickered with concern and he said, "Are you all right?" It—as well as his earlier wisecrack—was a throwback to the time when we were still together, and it gave me a displaced feeling.

"I'm fine," I said.

He nodded. Subject dismissed. "Tell me what happened." Now his tone was carefully neutral, his face expressionless. With a flash of relief, I realized he intended to treat me as if I were a stranger who had phoned in, and I was glad he'd adopted that attitude. It would make our dealings much easier.

I introduced him to Carolyn and explained why she had hired me. I went over my arrival at the hotel and what I had encountered. In the middle of this, the Vangs returned and added to the confusion. Mary Zemanek emerged from her apartment to see what the commotion was and immediately began invoking the owner's displeasure. Mr. Dinh, Hoa's father, identified his son's body, his pregnant wife standing by in stoical sorrow. She had, Carolyn said, lost two children on the flight from their homeland; while not inured to such loss, she could handle it better than most.

Finally the questioning was over. The lab men departed, and the coroner's personnel left with the body bag. Carolyn went upstairs with the Dinhs, saying we would reschedule our meeting with the Vangs tomorrow. Greg looked at me and said, "Shall I walk you to your car?"

"You don't have to—"

"It's no trouble."

We walked silently down the street toward the parking lot, the whores and derelicts giving us a wide berth, as if they sensed Greg was a cop. He placed his hand under my elbow—formally, the way he might guide a maiden aunt. Neither of us spoke until I had paid the attendant the parking fee and we were standing next to my car.

I said, "Thank you for walking me down here."

"That's okay." He paused. "Are you sure you're all right?"

"Yes. I wanted to ask you, though—can I remain on my case?"

Faint amusement flickered in his eyes. "Would it make any difference if I told you not to?"

58

"Yes, it probably would."

"It hasn't in the past."

I didn't want to dig up that particular bone of contention. "Look," I said, "that was a long time ago. I'm older now; people change with the years."

"Don't we." For a moment his eyes were far away. Then he said, "Sure, stay with it. I know you'll keep me posted on any important developments. And feel free to call me, if you need information."

"Thanks." I unlocked my car door.

He remained standing there, his hands in the pockets of his coat, blond hair gleaming in the rays from a nearby streetlight. "How have you been, anyway?"

"Pretty good. You?"

"The same. You still seeing that disc jockey?"

"Yes." I hesitated, and when he didn't say anything more, I asked, "What about you—are you seeing anybody?"

"Yeah, for about six months now. Nice lady, strategic planner with one of the big clothing firms. She travels a lot, but that's all right. I never had the opportunity to get used to someone who had dinner waiting on the stove every night."

"No, I guess you didn't."

Then he did a surprising thing: He leaned forward, put his hand on my shoulder, and kissed me lightly on the cheek. "Take care, will you?"

He squeezed my shoulder, turned abruptly, and walked out of the parking lot. I put my hand to my cheek and watched him go, amazed.

It was the damnedest thing, I thought. And what was even more surprising than the kiss was the other factor: Not once since he'd arrived at the hotel tonight had Greg called me by that insult to my one-eighth Indian ancestry, that godawful nickname he had for me—Papoose.

Now, sitting at Don's dining table and working on my third glass of wine, I still felt strangely suspended between different worlds. There was the world of the past, when Greg and I had been together; the world of the present and my comfortable life with Don. The violence of the Tenderloin, where human life was a cheap commodity; the security of this loft, where music and love were precious assets.

Confusion welled up inside me, and I knew it would soon be followed by tears. I'd better quit drinking, I told myself, and go to bed before I got maudlin.

I poured the rest of my wine down the sink, descended the stairs from the loft, and crossed to turn the lights off in the big central space. Then I climbed to the smaller loft, slipped out of my clothes, and crawled into the wide bed under the skylight. It was a clear night for December, and as I lay there on my back, I could see stars and high-flying wisps of cloud.

It was almost two in the morning. Right now they'd be taking last call for drinks at Don's favorite bar, the Blue Lagoon on Army Street, not far from the KSUN studios. The Lagoon had been a gay bathhouse before the AIDS epidemic; now it was converted to a bar with a tropical theme, and a heated courtyard with wrought-iron tables surrounded the Olympic-sized swimming pool. Don and the musicians he'd been interviewing would be sitting there by the turquoise water . . .

And then I was back at the Globe Hotel. In the basement. Kneeling next to Hoa Dinh's crumpled body, and all around me was the smell of death—

I jerked awake and turned over, bunching the pillows under my head. They smelled of Don, his talcum powder, the spray he used in an unsuccessful attempt to control his thick black hair. I hugged them closer, breathing in deeply, then turned my head and caught the orange numbers on the digital clock. A little after three.

They'd probably gone someplace to eat. Or to one of the many after-hours places Don knew. He'd be here soon. All I had to do was relax and sleep.

But the bloody images returned, and I tossed about. Come on, Don, I thought. Come home and hold me. Keep me away from that basement . . . from that body . . . from that other world where I don't want to be anymore . . .

60

— 9 —

When I climbed up to the kitchen loft the following morning, Don was at the stove frying eggs. He'd crawled into bed beside me around four o'clock, smelling of wine and stale cigarette smoke, and had been asleep before I could say more than hello. He'd had a restless sleep, though—full of tossing and mumbling—and now I could see why. From all appearances, Don had a magnificent hangover.

Now that was odd, I thought. Don liked to drink, but seldom anything stronger than red wine. And he never got hangovers.

I went over and gave him a good morning kiss. He reached around me and patted my rear. "How's the old war wound?" It was his ritual comment lately, referring to the bullet wound I'd suffered there on a recent case.

I was in no shape to think of a snappy comeback, so I merely took the plate he handed me and carried it to the table. "Rough night?" I said, sitting down and eyeing the eggs with distaste.

He smiled weakly and sat opposite me, coffee mug in hand. "Yeah."

"You're not eating?"

"No way, feeling like I do."

"Hmmm." I broke the egg yolk with my fork and began smearing it around on the plate. "You want to tell me about it?"

He sipped coffee and grimaced. "Where shall I start? Well, the taping with the Big Money Band went well. But then we went to the Lagoon for drinks. And that band is composed of hard-drinking old boys. Came up the rough and rowdy way—long tours, booze, drugs, you name it. I couldn't keep up with them. Didn't even try."

"Oh?" I looked him over skeptically.

"Well, maybe I tried a little. Anyway, long about last call, one of the boys decided to jump in the pool."

"Uh-oh." Swimming in the Blue Lagoon pool was strictly forbidden, and even a move in that direction was grounds for refusal of service.

"Yeah. That wouldn't have been so bad, but he decided to take Tony with him." Tony Wilbur is KSUN's program director and Don's boss. "Then," he went on, "another of them thought it was such a riot that *he* jumped in—carrying a waiter. Things got out of hand, and pretty soon there were twenty people in the pool and the cops were arriving."

"Where were you all this time?"

"Hiding under the table."

I grinned, picturing Don peering out through the white wrought-iron filigree. "And then?"

"The cops arrested everybody in the water, and I had to go to Potrero Station and straighten things out. Those old boys may have spent many a night in jail, but Tony hasn't. Besides, it wouldn't have looked good for KSUN, leaving them there. So duty called, and I went, and eventually everything got straightened out. End of story."

"I don't understand why you got stuck getting them released. Doesn't the station have a lawyer or a P.R. guy to handle things like that?"

Don rolled his eyes. "Yes, but our attorney wasn't available when I called him. And the P.R. guy was one of the ones in jail."

"Oh." I looked down at my uneaten eggs.

"You're not laughing," Don said. "Or eating your breakfast."

"I'm not hungry either."

"What's wrong? How come you're here, anyway? You told me you wanted to sleep at home last night, so you could get an early start this morning."

"I did, but something came up, and I decided it was better not to be alone."

He leaned forward, bushy eyebrows drawn together in a frown. "What happened?"

I set down my fork and told him about the murder at the Globe Hotel.

When I finished, Don was silent for a moment, stroking his mustache. "I'm sorry I wasn't here for you, babe," he finally said. "You know, sometimes your job makes mine look so goddamned frivolous."

"Don't feel bad. Right now I could do with a little frivolousness." Then, because he looked so downcast, I added, "Besides, not all the shows you do are lightweight. What about the one-in-four?" The one-in-four was the serious show Don did every month; he would pick an issue that was creating a major impact on the city and bring in people to discuss it. The show was live, with call-ins, and often provoked a good bit of controversy.

"One-in-four's not enough."

"Cheer up; it's a start." I pushed my plate away and stood up. "I'll call you later, okay?"

"Sure." He stood up too, eyes on my face. "Be careful, will you?"

"Look, it's broad daylight, and the sun's shining—what could happen to me? Like a lady at the Globe Hotel is fond of saying, 'There's nothing to be afraid of.'"

Don's frown returned. I could tell he didn't like the bitter tone in my voice. For that matter, neither did I.

Inspector Richard Loo was a slender Chinese who must have been around forty. In his correct blue pinstriped suit and wire-rimmed glasses, he looked more like a banker than a cop. He'd been with the SFPD's Gang Task Force since it was formed in the seventies in response to violence among the youth of Chinatown, and he was well known as an authority on all types of gangs—Oriental, Hispanic, black, or Caucasian. As I sat across the desk from Loo in his small cubicle at the Hall of Justice, I could see the keen intelligence in his bespectacled eyes and sense his toughness.

After leaving Don's, I'd gone home to let the contractor in, feed the cat, and change my clothes. Then I'd phoned All Souls for my messages. Loo had returned my call from the previous afternoon, saying he'd be in all morning, and since I had to make a formal statement about finding Hoa Dinh's body anyway, I'd driven directly to the Hall. The statement had taken only a short time, and I'd had to wait outside Loo's office for less than five minutes.

Now Loo said to me, "You're interested specifically in Vietnamese gangs?"

"Yes. I believe they're called 'the dust of life.'"

Loo nodded. "*Bui doi.* Somehow it's too passive a description for those types."

"Are there many such gangs active here in the city?"

"Hard to say. The Vietnamese gangs aren't as easy to pin down as, say, the Hispanics or Chinese. They're highly organized, but they're also highly mobile. They drift from city to city—probably that's where the term 'dust' comes from."

"I take it these aren't street gangs in the usual sense."

"No. It's hard to get a handle on them—or on what the typical member is like. The majority are young men, but others are in their forties. It's rumored that some of the older members may have been part of Nguyen Van Thieu's elite bodyguard corps. But that's just unconfirmed talk. They tend to confine their crimes to preying on their own people. Extortion. Robberies. Some of their schemes are pretty elaborate."

"Can you give me an example?"

"Blackmail. Protection. You remember that ethnic Chinese-Vietnamese couple who were tortured to death in the Richmond District last year? Or the couple who were gunned down in the Sunset?"

Vaguely I recalled reading about the cases in the paper. "Those were gang-related?"

"We suspect so, but again, it's hard to prove." Loo leaned back in his chair, the light from the overhead flourescents glinting off his glasses. "Our biggest problem in getting information or prosecuting gang members is the fear they engender in the Vietnamese community. Victims refuse to testify; or if they do, there are violent reprisals."

"What are the chances of a young man of sixteen being involved with one of these gangs?"

"Depends on the young man. If he was a drifter, alone in the country, it's very possible."

"The one I'm thinking of lived with his family in the Tenderloin. It seems a pretty stable home environment. He was studying electronics."

"Then it's doubtful he'd be involved with the *bui doi.*" Loo straightened up, placing his forearms on the desk. "Is the young man you're speaking of the one who was killed at the Globe Hotel last night?"

"Yes."

He motioned at a number of reports stacked on his blotter. "The details came up from Homicide an hour ago. I only glanced at them briefly."

"Well, I was hired to look into some incidents at the hotel and, in the process, found the boy's body."

"What sort of incidents?"

"Scare tactics. Nothing serious—until the murder."

Loo nodded, looking thoughtful. "So you think these incidents may be gang-related."

"It's a possibility."

"I'd say it's a remote one. The Tenderloin is relatively free of the kind of gang activity we're talking about. The reason for that being that the *bui doi* are primarily interested in money, and there isn't much to spare in those resettlement hotels. The gangs are more likely to hit on the well-off Vietnamese who have been here longer and are established, like those couples out in the Avenues."

It made sense, especially when coupled with what the grocer, Hung Tran, had said about Vietnamese gangs not being street gangs in the usual sense. Still, I was unwilling to completely let go of the idea. "The *bui doi* must live someplace, though, however temporarily, and I can't see them setting up in the Richmond or the Sunset. Wouldn't the Tenderloin be a logical place for them to locate?"

Loo shrugged.

I went on, "If they had surfaced in the Tenderloin and

someone at the Globe Hotel had gotten in the way of their activities . . ."

"Anything's possible." But the inspector looked doubtful.

I thanked him for his time and told him I'd report anything pertinent I might learn about Hoa Dinh and the *bui doi*. And the best place to start looking was into the life of the dead boy himself. His best friend, Duc Vang, should be able to supply some of the necessary details.

On the way to the hotel, I remembered the sheet I'd found in the basement storage locker the day before. The last I'd seen the sack containing it, it had been sitting where I'd put it next to the Christmas tree in the lobby. But in the commotion following the police's arrival, I'd forgotten it. I decided to look for it so I could show it to Duc.

But when I arrived at the hotel, Jimmy Milligan, the poetry lover who had confronted Brother Harry the day before, was hanging an ornament on the new live tree. It was a cheap silver-and-gold ball, and it clashed with the other handmade trimmings, but Jimmy didn't seem to notice. Mary Zemanek and the two Vietnamese toddlers who had been with her the previous day stood looking on, and they didn't seem to mind that the ornament wasn't up to par either.

When I came in, Jimmy turned to me, gestured at the tree, and said, "'Pardon, great enemy . . . without an angry thought . . . we've carried in our tree . . . and here and there have bought . . . till all the boughs are gay.'"

I said, "William Butler Yeats."

He smiled sadly at me. "'Upon a Dying Lady.' When her end is near, her friends bring her a Christmas tree. And rightly so. 'Tis the season. The great enemy, of course, is death . . ." His voice trailed off and he looked back at the tree with liquid brown eyes, his face as melancholy as a clown's. I wondered what past holiday scenes he was remembering.

Mary Zemanek said briskly, "That was a lovely thing to

bring an ornament, Jimmy. But you'd better run along now."

The bearded man roused himself from his reverie with an effort. "'And pluck, till time and times are done . . . the silver apples of the moon . . . the golden apples of the sun.'" He touched the ornament gently as he spoke, then moved toward the door.

When he had gone, I said, "What was all that about?"

Mary Zemanek sighed. "That poem—with the silver and golden apples in it—it's one of Jimmy's favorites. He recited the whole thing for me one time. It's about a man who catches a fish that turns into a girl and runs away from him. He spends his life looking for her."

"But doesn't find her?"

"That's Jimmy's way of seeing it. Who knows?" She paused, her pale eyes reminiscent. "You know, I used to read poetry when I was a girl. I've forgotten a lot of it, but I do remember my Yeats. Some of it is just beautiful, and I can recognize a number of the poems Jimmy recites."

"Really?" I was surprised at the sudden gentleness in her gravelly old voice.

"That one he was just reciting—about the apples—I've always thought it describes Jimmy's life. The opening line is something about going out into the hazelwood 'because a fire was in my head.' A fire, like the craziness in Jimmy's head. And it's about a search, only in Jimmy's case, it's a search for a home, not a girl."

I hadn't expected her to be so insightful. "Maybe he likes it for that reason."

"Maybe so." Then she looked at me curiously. "What's the name of that law firm you work for? Carolyn Bui mentioned it once, but I've forgotten."

"All Souls Legal Cooperative."

"That's odd."

"Yes, the name is a little strange for a law firm."

"No, I mean it's an odd coincidence. Jimmy's favorite poem lately is 'All Souls Night.' It's about ghosts drinking wine together, and mummies. It's eerie."

"I guess so." Although the wine part fit with All Souls. Or used to, I reminded myself, back in the days when it was full of convivial spirits. Maybe the part about the ghosts wasn't far off either. The place *did* have the feel of a subterranean crypt lately.

Mary looked over at the ornament on the tree. "Jimmy's a nice man," she said. "I hated to push him out, especially after he brought that ornament, but the owner wouldn't like him in here."

"Why? Jimmy isn't dangerous, is he?"

She glanced down at the two children, who were standing silently on either side of her, one clutching the skirt of her dress with a small hand. "You go back inside now," she told them. "Watch the TV until your mama comes."

The children went into her apartment, as quietly as they had disappeared the day before.

I asked, "Are you babysitting?"

"Yes. The mother has English classes until one." Mary came over to the counter and straightened the red cord that Jimmy's ornament was suspended from. She moved wearily, one hand pressed against her right side. When she turned, her pale eyes were puzzled. "Now what's this about Jimmy being dangerous?"

"I just wondered. He got into a fight with the street preacher, Brother Harry, yesterday."

"Oh, that. Happens all the time. Jimmy likes to needle the old goat. It's a game he plays."

"Harry doesn't seem to think it's a game."

"Well, no, he wouldn't. Man's got no sense of humor. Religious fanatics never do."

I had to agree with that. "How does Jimmy survive, anyway? Someone told me he won't go on welfare."

"He survives like any of them do. But I guess you wouldn't understand that." She looked scornfully at my six-year-old suede jacket, as if possession of it rendered me incapable of comprehending the difficulties of eking out a living in the Tenderloin. When I didn't reply, she went on. "Jimmy collects things from garbage cans; sometimes I give him odd jobs. And he panhandles. He once told me he can make ten dollars on a good day. And then there's the blood bank."

"He sells blood?"

"Twice a week, at three locations."

"Don't you have to be in good health to do that?"

She frowned, clearly annoyed. "Does Jimmy look like he's sick?"

"Well, no, but so many of the city's homeless people are either alcoholics or on drugs."

"Jimmy's neither. The man's a little cracked, but he lives right. Was raised that way."

"What way?"

"Christian. He once told me he was brought up in a good Catholic orphanage, plus lived in three foster homes. He knows better than to abuse his body like so many of them do."

And he also knew what it was to want a home, desperately. I felt a stab of sympathy for the young Jimmy Milligan.

Mary went on, "Jimmy makes sure to eat good—he's partial to fish and chips, when he has the money. And when he's got a home, he fixes it up nice."

"Where does he live now? I heard he got turned out of the last place."

"He's always getting turned out. And what's all this nosiness about Jimmy anyway?"

"It's part of my job."

Mary drew her lips into a stern line. "Your job? Your job is to find the lunatic who's been bothering us. Don't you try to put that on Jimmy. He's a good man, in spite of his oddness." She turned toward her apartment, then said, "Is there anything else, Miss McCone?"

"Just one thing. Last night I left a paper sack next to the Christmas tree. Have you seen it?"

"A sack?" She looked over at the tree.

"From Safeway. It had a sheet inside, an olive-green sheet."

69

An odd expression passed over her face, and then she said, "There was nothing here when the police finally left last night. If that sack was there, I would have seen it."

I watched her for a moment, then said, "Thanks," and moved toward the elevator. Behind me, I heard her apartment door slam.

I wasn't certain whether Mary was telling me the truth or not, but I was willing to bet she knew something about that sheet.

— 10 —

It was quiet in the hall outside the Vangs' apartment. No babies cried, no radios or TVs played. I looked at my watch and realized it was close to noon; probably the family was all working at their restaurant.

I knocked anyway and waited. The door opened, and Duc Vang looked out. His face, under the odd brushy haircut, was haggard and he seemed older than he had the day before. I noticed that his clothing—baggy blue pants and a loose smock—was more like that of the grocer, Hung Tran, than that of the other young Vietnamese men I'd seen on the streets. In attire, as in retention of his Vietnamese name, Duc seemed to prefer the old ways.

"No one is here but me," he said. "They are at the restaurant."

"Actually you're the one I want to talk to."

He nodded politely, displaying no surprise, and ushered me inside, indicating I should sit on the couch. He then perched on the arm at the opposite end and waited for me to speak.

"Duc," I said, "I'm very sorry about your friend Hoa Dinh."

He inclined his head slightly.

70

"The police," I went on, "are doing everything they can to find his killer. And since I'm here to find out who is causing the disturbances in this building, I can try to help them."

"Do you think this is one and the same person?"

"Possibly."

"I see."

"What can you tell me about your friend, Duc?"

"I don't understand."

"You and Hoa were good friends, isn't that true? Best friends?"

He hesitated. "Yes."

"How long had you known Hoa?"

"Since a year ago, when we came to this building."

"He was a good bit younger than you."

"Only five years. And he had had many terrible experiences. He was an adult."

"Terrible experiences getting out of Vietnam?"

"Both there and in this country."

"What kinds of things happened to him here?"

"The kind we all share. I cannot explain it."

I let it go for the moment. "Hoa was going to school, studying electronics?"

"Yes."

"Do you also go to school?"

"Not now. I work in the restaurant. My father wants me to attend college someday, but I am not sure I wish to."

"Why not?"

He shifted uncomfortably on the arm of the couch. "I do not see what your questions about me have to do with Hoa."

"I'm trying to get an idea of what Hoa's life was like. Sometimes the best way to do that is to ask about the lives of his close friends."

"I see."

This was getting nowhere. I tried another tack. "What sorts of things did you and Hoa and your other friends do together?"

"The usual things."

71

"Did you go to movies?"

"No."

"What about ballgames, or playing sports?"

Duc's lip curled slightly. "No. We are—were—not interested in sports."

"What, then?"

"We talked. We went about the neighborhood."

I'd seen a video game arcade around the corner, so I said, "What about video games? Did you play those?"

"No." He got off the couch and went to look out the window. It opened on an alley behind the building, a brick wall with similar windows only yards away.

"Why not? A lot of the people in the neighborhood enjoy them."

He was silent for a moment. "Hoa and I and our friends are not like those people."

"In what ways?"

There was an edge of annoyance in his voice when he said, "We do not play sports. Or video games. We do not go to movies. Or to the ballgames."

"Why not? Are those things so bad?"

He turned to face me. "Those things are for Americans, not for us."

I waited.

"Most of my people do not understand this," Duc finally added. "I cannot expect you to."

"Try to explain it to me."

It was as if I had broken through some reserve, one that was there simply because no one had ever troubled to ask him before. Duc came toward me, hands outstretched, gesturing. "I see this all the time. My people settle in America. They look around them, and suddenly they must *have*."

"Have what?"

"Everything." The gestures became more expansive. "Someone else has a television. Then the newcomer must also have a television. This one has a stereo. The newcomer must have a stereo as soon as he has saved a little money. My sisters—you have seen them. The designer blue

72

jeans, the T-shirts with stupid things written on them. Makeup. Hairdos. High heels. My parents are no better. They say we must save to move to the Sunset District. We must have a big house, and a car. They will fill the house with furniture and . . . and . . . things!" He flung his arms out wildly.

I said gently, "Isn't it natural that they would want to be as comfortable as they once were in Vietnam?"

"Comfortable, yes! But they choose the worst things about America to make their own. They are so anxious to fit in here. And in order to fit in, they must erase all the differences. They must erase who we really are."

"And who is that?"

"Vietnamese! We have a culture, an identity. And that is what they would throw away."

I thought of the Asian youths I saw driving their high-powered cars all over the city, rock-and-roll blaring from stereo tape decks. I pictured the Oriental families lined up in the catalog showroom I sometimes patronized, ordering huge quantities of merchandise that had been unheard of in their homelands. They did, at times, adopt the worst fads and fancies America had to offer.

I said, "So what did you and Hoa and the others plan to do about this?"

"Do?" Duc looked at me in surprise.

"I can tell from the way you dress that you aren't going along with the jeans and stupid T-shirts. And you tell me you don't go to the video arcades or the movies. But what were you doing instead?"

A strange look came over his face, and he turned back to the window. "I do not understand."

"I think you do. What I'm asking is my initial question—how did you and Hoa and the others spend your time?"

He was silent.

"You said you 'went about the neighborhood.' Doing what?"

After a moment he said, "We walked. We talked. We looked at the city, at what was happening here."

"And?"

"And what?"

"What did you think of what was happening here?"

His voice, when he spoke, was that of a small boy's. "We did not like it. We liked it less all the time. It made us want . . ."

"Yes?"

"It made us want to go home, to a land that is lost to us forever."

I couldn't get Duc to tell me anything more except for the names and apartment numbers of two other young men in the hotel who had been friends with Hoa Dinh. After I copied the information down, Duc excused himself, saying he had to go to work in the family restaurant. I climbed the fire stairs to the fifth floor, where Hoa's other friends lived, hoping to find them at home, but there was no response to my knocks. Then I thought of Sallie Hyde; given her maternal attitude toward the other residents, Sallie probably knew more about what went on in this hotel than anyone else.

Back on the fourth floor, I knocked at Sallie's door but got no answer. Of course—yesterday had been her day off, so today she would be working at her flower stand at Union Square. It was now after one; the noon rush would have subsided by the time I got there, and it would be a good time for us to talk.

Once downtown, I parked my car in the garage under Union Square and threaded my way across the crowded sidewalk to the curb opposite I. Magnin. Sallie's stand was diagonally across the intersection near the rival department store, Neiman-Marcus, and I could see her—swathed in bright green today—sitting on a stool inside it.

As I waited for the light, I glanced up at the towers of the St. Francis Hotel, where glass-enclosed elevators raced one another for the top. My eyes followed one down, and then I looked at the square itself. An old woman on a bench on the opposite side was feeding the pigeons, and great clouds of them swooped down at her feet. Well-dressed pedestrians hurried along the walks, ignoring a Salvation Army Santa who was stationed at their intersection, as well as the derelicts who lay on the grass soaking up the watery December sunlight. When the traffic cop's whistle sounded, I started across Geary Street toward the giant sugar cube of I. Magnin.

On the sidewalk in front of the department store a dancer in a red velvet suit—one of San Francisco's many street performers—whirled and spun, surrounded by a circle of shoppers. Three musicians—a banjo player, guitarist, and harmonica player—accompanied the man's graceful gyrations with a jazzed up version of "The Little Drummer Boy." He glided along, stopped in an abrupt pirouette just inches from a fat woman in a fur coat, then pivoted. Flinging out one long leg in a giant step, he danced off, red coattails flying. I paused to watch for a moment, then crossed Stockton and went up to Sallie's stand.

She was pinning a Christmas corsage of red and white carnations on a tourist lady, while the woman's male companion looked proudly on. Flashing me a gap-toothed grin, she pointed to the departing couple and said, "That's nice. They're on vacation, and he's doing something special for her. Makes both of them feel good."

"I guess that's the point of vacations," I said, remembering how Don had bought me a little pen-and-ink drawing of a country inn we'd stayed at in the Gold Rush country one weekend last fall. It now hung on the wall in my living room, and damned if it didn't make both of us feel good to look at it.

"So are you down here to do your Christmas shopping?" Sallie asked. "Or do you want to talk to me?"

I felt a faint pang of guilt about my undone shopping, but said, "I want to talk."

She waved me toward a stool inside the stand, and I sat, watching as she disciplined a bucket of daisies by plucking out the wilted blooms. Her hand hovered over a tub of long-stemmed roses, then dropped wearily to her side. "It's a terrible thing," she said, "to die that young."

"Hoa Dinh."

"Yes. Just the day before yesterday, I was telling his mother not to be afraid. What a fool I've been, to think these noises and mishaps were only pranks."

"Who did you think was playing the pranks?"

Before she could reply, a young man in a business suit tapped impatiently on the counter and pointed at the roses. Sallie turned to help him, selecting a bunch and wrapping them in pale green paper. After some deliberation, she chose a mauve ribbon with which to tie the conical package. When she turned back to me, her eyes were flashing.

"Hands me a pain," she said, "people who won't even bother to pick out their own flowers. Probably had a fight with his wife, is taking them to her as a peace offering. Poor woman—the marriage won't last. He doesn't even care if her roses are fresh."

I smiled, realizing she probably made her work time pass more quickly by making up stories about her customers.

Sallie sat down on a stool that was a companion of mine and reached for a portable radio that sat on the counter. She turned it up, listened, noted something on a paper, and then turned it down.

"I'm trying to win this contest," she said. "You write down all the songs they've played and when they say to, you call in. If you get through and tell them the right titles in order, you win a hundred bucks."

It was one of the many listener games KSUN played. "You listen to that station much?"

"All the time. The music isn't much, but the d.j.'s are really something."

"The reason I asked is that my boyfriend works there. Don Del Boccio."

Sallie's fleshy face lit up. "Old Devastating Don? He's your boyfriend?"

"Yes."

"I listen to him all the time. He's got a terrific sense of humor."

I felt a flash of pride. "He *is* pretty good, isn't he?"

"I love him. A lot of people in the neighborhood do. KSUN's real popular in the Tenderloin, for some reason. Maybe all the giveaway games they play."

Now that she mentioned it, I'd noticed the distinctive sounds of KSUN blaring out in a number of places down there. I'd have to report this phenomenon to Don. To Sallie, I merely said, "I'll tell Don you like him; he'll be pleased. But back to the problems at the hotel—who did you think might be playing pranks?"

She reached for a container of violets. "The boys, of course."

"You mean Hoa and Duc and the others in the hotel?"

She nodded, selecting some violets and leaves.

"Aren't they a little old to be called boys?"

"Yes and no." Sallie arranged the flowers against the leaves, then deftly began fastening their stems together with wire. "In their years, they're men. In experience of a certain type—the war, things like that—they've matured far beyond their age. But those boys missed their childhood. Now that they're safe in this country, they're having it."

"I didn't meet Hoa, and I haven't had a chance to talk with the others, but Duc strikes me as a very angry and alienated young man."

"That's part of the childishness. He feels out of place here and so he rebels and refuses to fit in." Sallie pulled a length of white ribbon off a roll and began to tie a bow.

"He puts it on a cultural basis," I said, "says he doesn't want to lose his Vietnamese identity."

She nodded. "Of course he says that. It's an excuse for the fact that he refuses to grow up and make a life for himself. He can make his way in this country without losing touch with his heritage—and underneath, he knows it."

"Was Hoa the same way?"

"Yes, Hoa and the rest of them. They banded together and cried on each other's shoulders."

"What else did they do, when they weren't feeling sorry for themselves?"

77

"Not much. I'd find them sitting in the stairwell with long faces on, smoking and talking."

"Smoking . . . ?"

"Tobacco, not marijuana. In spite of their not wanting to grow up, they're not bad boys. They're confused, that's all. Confused, like we've all been."

"So you thought they were playing pranks because they were bored and at loose ends?"

"Yes. Boys, you know, will be boys, no matter what country they were born in."

"But now you don't think they were the ones who were causing the trouble."

"No." Sallie finished the corsage and held it up for me to admire, but her eyes were bleak. "No, I don't."

"Why not?"

"It's obvious, isn't it? They're good boys. They wouldn't kill their friend."

"What if they'd gotten involved with some bad companions—"

A tall, classically beautiful woman in a blond fur jacket came up with a bunch of white orchids. Sallie wrapped them, money changed hands, and the woman walked off, smiling down at the flowers.

"She's a regular," Sallie said. "A model at Saks. Looks happier than usual today; probably she's having her boyfriend over for a special dinner."

Momentarily sidetracked, I said, "Do you *know* she has a boyfriend?"

Sallie looked surprised. "A woman like that? Of course she's got a boyfriend! He's probably some sort of business tycoon, or maybe a movie producer, going to take her to Hawaii for Christmas."

I smiled, amused at her inventiveness. "Anyway," I said, "what if Hoa and the others had been keeping bad company?"

"You mean with criminals?"

"Yes."

"There aren't any criminals living in the hotel."

"But outside . . . ?"

She frowned, clearly disturbed at the notion. "I wouldn't know about that. I try to avoid those types."

"Who would know?"

"Well . . ." She fingered a curl of white ribbon hanging from one of the spools. "I suppose you could talk to Mr. Tran, the grocer on the corner. He sees pretty much everything that goes on on the street."

I had asked Hung Tran about the Vietnamese street gangs, but not about other criminal activity. Perhaps he could be of help to me after all. "What about the neighborhood characters—Brother Harry, for instance? Have you ever seen him around the hotel, acting suspicious?"

"No. I see him up on the corner near that porno theatre every day. And sometimes at a cafeteria where I eat. But not around the hotel." She paused, a strange expression on her face. "But thinking of Harry makes me think of the guy who runs that theatre."

"Otis Knox."

"Yes. Now, *he's* someone I've seen around the hotel. Saw him there a couple of days ago, sitting in the stairwell with the Vang girl."

A lot of activity seemed to center on that stairwell. I said, "Which one of the Vang daughters?"

"Dolly, the youngest. She's only fifteen, and I wondered about her being alone with a man like Otis Knox. I meant to speak to her about him, warn her to keep her distance. But I wanted to catch her alone so I wouldn't embarrass her." Sallie paused, looking thoughtfully at me. "Maybe you could talk to her? Tell her he's not suitable company?"

"No," I said, "I'll do better than that. I'll talk to Otis Knox."

I. Magnin has one of the most sumptuous powder rooms in the world, and it always makes me feel slightly regal to enter it. That afternoon, however, I barely glanced at the elegant ladies draped on the luxurious chairs—and I certainly didn't bother to examine my image in the many mirrors, because I suspected it would look haggard and unkempt. Instead, I crossed to the bank of telephones—the reason I had come up there—and looked up the number of the Sensuous Showcase Theatre.

The woman who answered told me Mr. Knox wasn't in. When I pressed her, claiming urgent business about an insurance policy that had lapsed, she said he was making the rounds of the other theatres and then would be going home for the day. She refused to give me either his home telephone number or the address of his ranch.

Somewhat deflated, I got out another dime and called Carolyn Bui at her office. Sounding harried, she said she was just going in to a meeting with her board of directors. They were upset about the murder at the Globe Hotel and seemed to hold her personally responsible for settling refugees in a place where they could get killed. Carolyn wanted to talk with me later about how the investigation was progressing and suggested we have dinner. I told her I wasn't sure I could make it, but would check in later.

After I hung up the phone I stood staring at it for a minute, then turned and caught my reflection in the mirror. My slacks were rumpled, my hair streamed down in an unruly mass, and my worn suede jacket showed every one of its six years. Out of the corner of my eye, I could see one of the elegant ladies watching me, clearly wondering what I was doing in a high-toned department store powder room.

Ordinarily it would have amused me, but right now I wanted to go over and shake her, to tell her that she had no business being so smug. After all, *she'd* never had to support herself, never had to work long hours at a demanding and emotionally exhausting job, never had to find a boy's broken body in the basement of a Tenderloin hotel.

Of course, I didn't go over to her. Instead I retrieved my car from the parking garage, and drove across town to Bernal Heights and All Souls. It was time, I had decided, to confront Hank about the future of my demanding job.

— 11 —

There were no parking spaces on either side of the grassy triangular park that divided the street in front of All Souls, and a white Volvo sat in the driveway. After cruising around unsuccessfully for five minutes, I parked parallel across the drive and left a note at Ted's desk, saying I would be in Hank's office if the Volvo's owner wanted me to move. Then I went down the hall, ignored the Do Not Disturb sign, and knocked on Hank's door.

An irritated growl came from within, and I entered. My boss sat behind his cluttered desk, wearing one of the plaid woodsman's shirts he favored these days, his Brillo pad of light brown hair looking badly in need of a trim. When he saw me, he growled some more, took off his horn-rimmed glasses, and began to polish them on the tail of his shirt. His eyes, without the thick lenses, looked like a tired little boy's.

I said, "Do you have a few minutes?"

He hesitated, then gestured at one of the client's chairs. "Where have you been for the last few days?" he asked. "I haven't seen you around."

"It's hard to see somebody when you've always got your door closed."

He ignored that, inspecting the lenses of his glasses and then putting them back on. "Are you still working on the Globe Hotel job? I saw that someone was killed there."

Of course he would know all about it; Hank read our two daily papers—as well as those of several other major cities—with microscopic attention to detail. And if they hadn't told him enough, he could always have called his close friend Greg Marcus for further information.

"Yes, I'm still on it," I said, and filled him in on what I'd been doing.

When I finished, Hank said, "Well, stay with it as long as the client wants you to. And keep me informed how it's going."

I waited, then realized it was a dismissal. Hank was not going to speculate with me as to motive or killer; he was not going to warn me to keep up with my other duties for the co-op; he was not even going to tease me about my encounter with Greg, or throw out sly comments about the lieutenant and me getting back together someday. This was not the Hank Zahn I'd known since we were both in college, and his new manner scared me even more than the tense silence that had fallen over All Souls.

I started to get up, but then sat back down again. Hank looked at me, and I could see both annoyance and relief in his eyes. He knew what was coming.

I said, "Isn't it time you told me what's going on?"

He began to straighten a pile of papers that lay in front of him. "What do you mean?"

"You know very well what I mean." I began ticking items off on my fingers. "Almost everybody's moved out of the rooms upstairs. You're always hiding in your office. Someone's intimidated Ted so much that he's afraid to do his crossword puzzles. I'm getting cranky notes about leaving my car in the driveway. Good Lord, there's not even any food in the refrigerator!"

Hank smiled faintly. "I can see where that would pose a problem for someone of your, er, gastronomic abilities."

"Hank, that's not the point and you know it. There are no *people* here anymore! There's no *life!* Something bad is happening to All Souls, and I have a right to know what."

He took off his glasses and began polishing them again, apparently forgetting he had just completed that delaying exercise. After about fifteen seconds of watching him, I got up, reached across the desk, and snatched the glasses out of his hand. He stared at me, then tried to snatch them back. I moved away where he couldn't reach them.

"What in God's name has come over you?" he said.

"I want to talk about what's going on here."

82

"I know that, but how can I talk when I can barely see you?"

"I'll give you back your glasses on one condition—that you put them on your nose where they belong and quit using them as a way to avoid the issue."

He sighed and held out his hand.

I gave him the glasses and returned to my chair. "Now," I said.

Hank leaned forward, his strong, lean hands laced together on top of the pile of papers. He started to speak, hesitated, and then said, "I don't know how much longer All Souls is going to exist."

It jolted me. I sat back, shaken. I had expected something bad—but nothing so final as this.

"What's happened," he went on, "is that we've developed two factions among the partners. There are the newer people who've joined in the last few years. And there are the old hands like me, who founded the co-op."

I started to remind him that he alone had founded All Souls, but then stopped. It was characteristic of him to give joint credit to the others, who had lent support—and often money—during those first hard years.

"The new people," Hank said, "want to take All Souls in a different direction, get rid of what they call our 'sixties image.' The rest of us are willing to make some changes, but not everything they're insisting on."

"What kind of changes do they want to make?"

"Do away with the sliding fee scale. Start paying competitive salaries to our attorneys. Move the offices to a better location. A few people even feel the name is outmoded."

"But that's changing *everything!*"

"I know." He gestured wearily.

"Well, what *are* you willing to go along with?"

"Oh, I think that we should spiff the building up, create better office space. But I can't see moving downtown or to one of those office parks down in Daly City—as has been suggested. We located here in Bernal Heights because it was convenient for our clients. A lot of them live nearby;

many are too poor to own a car and too busy to hassle with a long trip downtown on the Muni. I'll be damned if I'm going to make it more difficult for them to reach us!"

Two flushed spots had appeared on Hank's cheeks. I took them as a positive sign.

"As for abolishing the sliding fee scale," he went on, "that's unacceptable. This co-op was founded on the principle of providing good, low-cost legal service for people who otherwise couldn't afford it. They pay according to their income; if you take that away, you negate the reason for us existing. I'm not saying I wouldn't go for an increase in the fees—that's only reasonable, given the increases in our costs. And I'm willing to stretch the budget for higher salaries and better benefits. After all, we've got to live too."

Hank paused, obviously hearing how loud his voice had risen, then started speaking again, lowering it in volume but not in intensity. "Dammit, Shar, none of the original partners joined All Souls with the idea of getting rich. We *knew* salaries wouldn't be competitive. We knew benefits wouldn't be lavish. But we joined together anyway—because we wanted to help people. We wanted to do right by our fellow man." He laughed bitterly. "Help people. Do right. I guess we *are* outmoded."

It reminded me of the thoughts I'd had on the roof of the Globe Hotel the day before—about being out of step with the eighties. I said, "Just a bunch of aging radicals, huh?"

"That's us." He smiled painfully, but there was a certain pride in the words. Hank wore three-piece suits to court now; he preferred the symphony to rock concerts; he drank good Scotch rather than Ripple wine. But he could never forget what it had been like on the battlefields of Vietnam—or on the protest lines after he had returned. He believed in those abstract concepts of helping people and doing right. And because of that I felt easier about the future of All Souls.

I said, "By 'us,' do you mean people like Anne-Marie?"

"Yes, she's one who's on my side. She moved out because she couldn't both work and live in this oppressive

84

atmosphere, but she's still solidly behind me. So are Harold and Walt and Michele."

"And the other side—they're people like Gilbert Thayer?"

"Yes. In fact, he's the ringleader."

I thought of the note Gilbert had left on my car the previous afternoon, telling me not to park in the driveway. And then I pictured Gilbert himself—a slender young man with a lounge-lizard mustache, prominent teeth, and a sour expression that made him look like a dyspeptic rabbit.

"You should see your face," Hank said.

"Well, I've never liked Gilbert. You've got to admit, both in looks and disposition, he's one of your more unappetizing specimens."

"His ideology bothers me far more than his temperament or looks. People like Gilbert have always existed in the profession, but it's a breed I'll never understand. And we're seeing more and more of them coming out of the law schools lately. They don't see the law as a framework for protecting the individual's rights; instead they consider it a system under which a few—primarily themselves—can benefit. And within that system, the ordinary client is little more than a revenue-producing unit."

He was right—and that was even more scary than the possible demise of All Souls. "Hank," I said, "I still don't see how people like Gilbert can just walk in here and try to take control."

"They're not just walking in, Shar. They're partners."

"But you and Anne-Marie and the others—you've been here longer. Don't you have seniority?"

"No. And I suppose that's my fault. It's ironic, too—Gilbert and his supporters are accusing me of living back in the sixties, when actually it was my attempt to bring All Souls into the eighties that put power in their hands in the first place."

"I don't understand."

"A few years ago I decided we needed to offer fuller services to our clients. Oh, we had a few specialists, like

Anne-Marie on tax law, but basically we didn't have the expertise our clients needed. So I set out to recruit people with those specialties—Gilbert on contract law, for instance. And I quickly found out that my colleagues are more money-oriented now than they were when we graduated. I couldn't afford most established professionals, so I had to recruit from the law schools. And even with new graduates, I had to offer more than a low salary, a room on the second floor, and a lot of job satisfaction. What I ended up offering was full partnerships."

"You mean people like Gilbert have as much say in what happens around here as *you* do?"

"That's it."

Once again, he'd stunned me. And suddenly I had a horrible suspicion. "Hank," I said, "if Gilbert's faction has its way, what do they intend to do about my job?"

He looked uncomfortable.

"Hank!"

"They want to contract with an outside agency. They claim we don't have enough work to support an on-staff investigator."

I thought of the ten- and twelve-hour days I routinely put in. I thought of the witnesses I interviewed, the court cases I testified in, the documents I delivered or filed. I thought of the cases I'd solved that had put All Souls' name on the front page of the newspapers and brought new clients to our door.

"I know," Hank said gently.

"You know! Is that all you can say—you *know?*"

There was a knock on the door, then it burst open so hard it banged into the wall. Gilbert Thayer—the devil we'd been speaking of—stood there, his little mustache twitching indignantly. "Sharon," he said, "you've parked so I can't get out of the driveway!"

So that was who owned the white Volvo. "I'll be with you in a minute, Gilbert," I said, reaching for my keys and turning back to Hank.

Gilbert remained standing there, breathing wheezily. I glanced back. "I said I'll be right with you."

"Sharon," he said, "I left you a note yesterday about using the driveway."

"I'm not in the driveway, Gilbert. I'm in the street."

Damned if the corners of Hank's mouth didn't quirk up.

"Nonetheless," Gilbert said stuffily, "the driveway is not for your convenience."

It was the same phrase he had used in his note. The driveway, according to Gilbert, was for the *convenience of the attorneys only.* I began to smile, wickedly.

Hank looked puzzled.

"Gilbert," I said, "where do you live?"

"At Potrero Towers. You know that." The Towers was a luxury condominium complex where, as Gilbert was fond of telling anyone who would listen, his father had bought him a unit.

"I see. And whose convenience is the driveway for?"

Now Hank began to smile, with a wickedness that matched my own.

Gilbert, however, was so caught up in his self-righteous anger that he didn't realize his error. "Sharon, I need to get out of here. Now, will you move your car!"

"According to your note to me yesterday, the driveway is for the convenience of the attorneys—but it's really for the residents. I believe that's written into the house rules. It's never been enforced, because people realize parking is tight, and they try to get along and make one another's lives easier."

"Still, it is a rule—"

"Gilbert, *you're* in violation of it, then. You're not a resident."

There was a long silence behind me. When I looked over my shoulder at him, his bunny-rabbit face was absolutely still.

"You're no more a resident here than I am, Gilbert," I said. "Since you do not choose to live here, the driveway is not for your convenience either."

An ugly red tinge began to spread over his face. His nose and mustache twitched furiously. I wished I had a carrot to feed him.

Finally he said, "You . . . you . . . you move your car!"

"Sorry, Gilbert." I turned to Hank. Hank had one hand pressed against his forehead and was staring at the pile of papers in front of him. His shoulders were shaking.

"I'll have it towed!" Gilbert said. "I will, I'll have it towed, you're blocking a driveway, it's illegal, I'll have it towed!"

Suddenly Hank snorted. I stared at him in amazement. He snorted again.

Sometimes, in moments of social duress, when I know I should control my mirth but can't, I let forth with embarrassing sounds that resemble a pig rooting in its trough. I had often caused Hank discomfort by doing so, but now it appeared he finally understood the impulse.

"Move that car!" Gilbert shouted. "You move that car right now!"

"Sorry, Gilbert."

"The police, I'll call 911!"

"The number to call to have a car towed is 553-1631, Gilbert."

The door slammed as Gilbert departed.

It took a moment for Hank to get himself under control. When he finally did, he said, "Aren't you worried about your car?"

"Nope. It's nearly four o'clock, the time they start clearing the tow-away zones. It will take them at least an hour to even get a cop out here."

Hank took off his glasses and wiped tears of laughter from the corners of his eyes. "Jesus Christ," he said, "the guy really puts you in a fighting mood, doesn't he?"

"Yes. You?"

"Yes." He grinned across the desk at me, and once more I felt the camaraderie we'd always shared—employer and employee but, more important, friend and friend. The way we'd been for years; the way All Souls had been too.

Hank said, "I haven't had a really good battle with anybody in quite a while. To tell you the truth, I'm kind of looking forward to the one that's coming up."

— 12 —

There was no sign of Gilbert when I went down the hall toward my office, but Ted was at his desk, typing with a jauntiness I hadn't seen him exhibit in months. He motioned to me and said, "Bugs Bunny put in a call to have your car towed."

"I kind of thought he would."

"When he stormed outside to wait for the cops, I canceled the tow order."

"Thanks, Ted. I owe you a beer."

"It was my pleasure."

He went back to his typing and I went to my office and called my house to check on Barry, the contractor. He had been there, waiting to get in, when I'd returned home to change my clothes that morning. Now there was no answer. Perhaps, I told myself, he was too busy to pick up the phone. But I had to admit that didn't sound like Barry. Next I called Carolyn Bui. She was still meeting with her Board of Directors, her secretary informed me. I hung up the receiver and slumped in my ratty old armchair, reflecting that I wasn't the only one having difficulty at my place of work.

My place of work. I looked around the tiny cubicle, with its sharply slanting ceiling and pale yellow walls that no amount of decoration had been able to make attractive. This office was really a converted closet; my salary was dismally low; there were few fringe benefits. If Gilbert's faction won out in the struggle for control of All Souls and my job ceased to exist, I could get a job with one of the big agencies in town. I had a certain reputation and—even though part of it said I was unorthodox and unresponsive to authority—I knew there were a couple of outfits where I could pretty much write my own ticket. What would I be losing, anyway? A closet for an office and a paycheck that never stretched far enough.

Wait a minute, an inner voice told me. For one thing, you'd be losing your freedom. There is—or at least there used to be—a warmth and companionship here, and they also leave you alone.

But, I reminded myself, there would be extra money for the house renovation. And paid vacations. Maybe even a dental plan. Or a pension.

What about a sense of purpose? the annoying voice asked. You feel like you're doing something valuable here, something that counts.

Does it? I thought. Sometimes I wonder. That's the trouble with getting older. You start entertaining basic doubts about how much you're accomplishing. And things like pensions and dental plans begin to matter more than ideals.

Restlessly I got up and left the office, wandering down the hall to the living room at the back of the house. It was deserted, and I stood in front of the window, watching the play of wintry sunlight on the tangle of vegetation in the backyard. There was a brick-and-board bookcase under the window for the convenience of the clients who waited in that room for their appointments, as well as for the leisure reading of the residents. The books were well-worn, most of them donated by the attorneys, many looking like supplemental texts from long-forgotten college courses. I ran my fingers over them, aligning the spines an even inch from the edge of the shelf, and as I did so, I encountered a volume of Yeats' poetry. Thinking of Jimmy Milligan, I pulled it out and leafed through it until I found "All Souls Night."

As Mary Zemanek had said, the poem was eerie, all about wine glasses brimming with muscatel and ghosts coming to drink at midnight. I could picture a room straight out of a horror film: draped in cobwebs, deep in shadow, where spirits of the long-dead came to commune. Shivering, I turned the pages and read Jimmy's other favorite, "The Song of Wandering Aengus." It wasn't very cheerful either, but at least it didn't give me gooseflesh. Yeats seemed to have had a gloomy preoccupation with death; a number of his stanzas that ended in italicized lines dwelled on it: *"She was more beautiful than thy first love, But now lies under boards"* . . . *"All things remain in God"* . . . *"And there the king is but as the beggar"* . . . *"What shall I do for pretty girls now my old bawd is dead?"*

Dammit, what was I doing reading poetry when I had a murder to investigate? I shut the book, put it back on the shelf, and located the living room phone by following its twenty-five-foot cord down the hallway to where the instrument sat outside the restroom. Red push-button phones with long cords were an All Souls tradition—one that caused more confusion than convenience, owing to the residents' practice of wandering while talking and then abandoning the phones wherever they were when they hung up.

I sat crosslegged on the hallway floor and punched in the number of the Sensuous Showcase Theatre. No, the woman there told me, Mr. Knox had not returned before going home. And no, she still could not give me the phone number at the ranch.

I hung up and thought of Knox's insistence that he was just a country boy at heart. He'd said, "By nightfall, I'm back home with my horses." Home, on his ranch in Marin County. Nicasio, he'd said.

It was now four-thirty and the first wave of commuters would be creeping across the Golden Gate Bridge and up the Waldo Grade into Marin County. Buses would be whizzing along in the special lanes allotted for them on the southbound side of the freeway, but traffic would still be slowed to a crawl by the time I reached San Rafael and the exit I needed to take for Nicasio. I wanted to talk to Otis Knox, though, and I could brood as well in traffic as in my office.

I was leery of going out to Knox's ranch without leaving word of my whereabouts, so I scribbled a short note to Hank, telling him he should contact the Marin County Sheriff's Department if I didn't check in with him by nine that evening. After slipping it under his office door, I left the building, circumventing Gilbert, who was now in the law library, throwing a tantrum about police inefficiency.

The Nicasio Valley lies in the western part of Marin County, pocketed in the section between San Rafael and the sea. It is long and narrow, surrounded by lightly wooded hills and dotted with cattle and horse ranches. By the time I reached it, dusk had fallen, and the lights of ranch buildings shone faintly through thick stands of oak, madrone, and eucalyptus. Just outside the little village for which the valley is named, a knobby hill reared up, its rocky outcroppings and stunted trees casting eerie shadows in the fading light.

The village centered on a square, most of which was a softball diamond. Across the road to one side was a white country church with a red roof and steeple, and directly ahead of me was a group of frame buildings that housed the post office and a restaurant. The post office would be closed by now, but perhaps someone at the restaurant could tell me how to find Otis Knox's ranch.

I was already stopped in the parking lot when I realized the place was deserted. There were no other cars, and the only light was the red beacon on the volunteer fire department up the road. The restaurant must either be closed for good or for the slow winter season when few people ventured out for drives in the hills of West Marin. I put the car in reverse, backed up, and continued around the deserted square.

On its third side were a couple of houses, a realty office, an antique store, and an odd humped-backed building called the Druids' Hall. All the businesses were dark and closed up. A few yards past them, the road curved sharply in front of a house with big trees and a white picket fence. As I braked and made the turn, I reflected that it would take a braver person than I to live there, what with the headlights of every car sweeping over my front windows and the imminent possibility of one veering out of control and ending up in my living room.

At the end of the curve, I found myself back at Nicasio

Valley Road, where I'd come in. I paused there, then decided to ask questions at one of the houses on the other side of the square. After turning left, I drove along its perimeter once more, past the old church to the intersection near the post office. I was about to turn again when I spotted a pair of headlight beams coming around the corner from where the main road branched off again to the west. A mud-splattered white pick-up truck drove into the parking area in front of the post office, and a man got out carrying some letters.

By the time he turned back from the mailbox, I had pulled in beside his truck and gotten out. He was a big bearded man in work clothes and heavy boots, and he stopped, shading his eyes from the glare of my headlights. I crossed to him, pulling my jacket tight against the unexpectedly chill air.

"Help you, lady?" The man's voice held soft country accents.

"I hope so. I'm trying to locate a ranch near here; it belongs to a man called Otis Knox."

"Knox? Name's not familiar. He in cattle or horses?"

"Horses, I think."

The man considered, then said, "I breed Arabians myself, and I don't know anyone named Knox. Is it a big spread?"

"Probably not too big."

Again he paused, then shook his head. "Doesn't ring a bell. Sorry I can't help you."

Inwardly I chided myself for coming out here without more information. Of course Otis Knox, porno king, was not about to advertise his presence in this conservative ranching country. Still, anyone as eccentric as he would surely have attracted some attention . . .

"Wait a second," I said. "This ranch is a little strange. The fellow collects things. He's got a pair of golden arches from McDonald's—"

"Oh, sure, *that* place. Folks call it Junk Food West. Guy's some kind of crazy millionaire, a movie producer, they say. Likes his privacy. Otis Knox is his name?"

"Yes. Can you tell me how to get there?"

"Sure can." He led me around his pick-up truck and pointed back the way I'd come. "You follow Nicasio Valley Road down to the fork; it's just a little ways. Bear left, onto Lucas Valley Road, maybe half a mile. The place is on the right, over a wooden bridge. You can see them arches, right through the trees."

I thanked him, got in my car, and drove as he'd directed me. Lucas Valley Road was easy to find, but there were a number of places set back on the opposite side of a small creek, and many of them could be reached by wooden bridges that spanned the gully. I followed the road for two miles, then doubled back, peering into the thick woods for Knox's golden arches. It was full dark now, and I could see little more than the glimmer of distant lights beyond the trees.

When I reached the fork where the roads came together, I turned and started back. Otis Knox, the "movie producer," liked his privacy; it would stand to reason that he would not put his name on his mailbox. His neighbors, on the other hand, seemed fond of large stylized lettering and elaborately carved signs.

I drove slowly, looking for an unmarked private road, and when one appeared about three-quarters of a mile from the fork, I turned in and rumbled over the rustic bridge. The drive wound through a stand of eucalyptus and then came out in flat pastureland. The dark shadows of the arches rose incongruously in front of a sprawling ranch house with flagstone facing around the front entry. I had barely stopped the car when floodlights came on, illuminating the arches in all their gaudy yellow splendor.

A black Ford Bronco was parked between the arches. By the time I pulled up next to it and got out of the MG, the door of the house had opened and Otis Knox stepped out. He was dressed, as before, in cowboy garb, and cradled a rifle in his arms. His stance, while easy, was alert. One careful fellow, this Mr. Knox.

When he saw who I was, he relaxed slightly. "Hey, honey," he called, "you came to meet Babe the Blue Ox."

94

"I sure did."

"Had quite a job finding me, I bet."

I nodded.

"But you managed anyway."

"Of course—I *am* a detective."

When I came up to him, Knox took one hand off the rifle and shook mine. In spite of his light words, his expression was wary. I smiled, trying to put him off his guard, and he smiled back, but the warmth didn't touch his eyes. "How do you like my golden arches?" he asked.

"They're very impressive. How'd you get them here?"

"Flatbed truck."

"Must have caused quite a stir among your neighbors."

"It had them wondering." Abruptly he turned and started for the house. "Come on, I'll show you the rest of the place."

The exterior of the house—with the exception of the arches—was what you might see in any affluent suburb, but the interior looked like the playroom of a mad child. The slate-floored entry was filled with the kind of coin-operated machines that give forth with gumballs or plastic prizes, and in the archway between it and the living room stood a mechanical bull. The only normal object in the living room was a grouping of low, modular couches and chairs upholstered in a deep red. The rest was a mélange that made the decor I'd seen in Knox's office seem tame.

Along the left-hand wall was a bar with stools that reproduced an old-fashioned ice cream parlor. Opposite it, five jukeboxes of various vintages lined up against the right-hand wall. There was a red-and-gold popcorn cart on wheels, half full of popped kernels; an ancient Coca-Cola machine; a three-foot-high statue of Donald Duck that apparently would quack at you if you fed it a quarter; an equally tall green ceramic frog that sat open-mouthed beside one of the modular chairs; and a pinball machine, 1950s model. Over all of this, darting silver lights flashed, and when I looked up I saw a mirrored globe that once must have hung in a ballroom.

Knox had set down the rifle and was watching me expectantly. "Well, what do you think?"

"I'm stunned."

He nodded. "Most people are. But now for the *pièce de resistance*." He crossed the room and pulled open the drapes that covered the back wall. A picture window overlooked the pastureland behind the house, with a stable and paddocks in the foreground and the looming shape of the mountains beyond. And dominating this pastoral scene was the floodlit figure of Babe the Blue Ox.

Babe was enormous, at least a dozen feet tall. His flanks bulged out as if he'd eaten all the cheeseburgers and fries the defunct Paul Bunyan Drive-in in Corvallis, Oregon, had ever served up. His fat cheeks puffed in bovine contentment. His eyelids drooped languidly. He was very blue. Not baby blue, or powder blue, or even just ordinary blue-blue. No, Babe was electric blue. Blue as the bluest neon sign.

"Good Lord," I said.

Knox smiled, obviously taking my words as an expression of admiration. "Something, isn't he?"

"Something."

He closed the drapes again and came toward me. "Hey, sit down, relax. You want a beer?"

"I could certainly use one."

He went over to the Coke machine and fed it a slug from a bowl that sat on top of it. What came out was Stroh's. He got another, opened them, and handed one to me. Then we went to the grouping of furniture and sat down opposite one another. Knox reached in his shirt pocket for a cigarette and matches, and when he had waved the match out, he put it into the mouth of the ceramic frog.

"The frog's supposed to be a plant holder," he said, "but I don't like crap like plants. So I use it for an ashtray."

I merely shook my head in amusement. Knox, with his boyish enthusiasm for his toys, seemed a harmless eccentric, and I took a long sip of beer while I reminded myself that in actuality he was a dangerous man. Knox was a ruthless operator in an industry that—much as he liked to portray it as sort of a home for wayward girls—routinely destroyed lives and people. I shifted my beer to my left hand and let my right one stray to the comforting bulge my .38 Special made in the outside pocket of my shoulder bag. While I normally didn't believe in carrying the gun, tonight was one of those occasions when I felt safer with it.

Knox was watching me now, the wary light back in his eyes. "So what do I owe the honor of this visit to?" he said. "You didn't come all the way out here just to meet Babe."

"No."

As I'd hoped, he quickly supplied his own perception of my motives. "You want to talk some more about those old boys—Brother Harry and Jimmy Milligan."

"Yes. I'm even more interested in what goes on in that neighborhood now. You've heard about the murder at the Globe Hotel?"

"Oh, yeah. One of the slopes. Too bad." He swigged beer, unconcerned.

I controlled my flaring anger and said, "Yes, it *was* too bad. And I'd think you'd be a little more worried."

"Why?"

"Well—what if the killer is the man who preaches in front of your theatre every day?"

Knox shrugged. "Honey, there are killers all over the Tenderloin. They bump people off in bar brawls, or while they're mugging bag ladies, or rolling drunks. They push adulterated dope. Sometimes we're lucky and they bump themselves off instead. But it's a way of life there."

"What if this killer has more of a motive than just random violence?"

"This killer? You mean Harry?"

"Maybe."

"What motive would old Harry have?"

"That's what I'm hoping you can tell me."

"Me? Honey, I'm just—"

"I know; you're just a country boy. You don't know anything about what goes on in the neighborhood, in spite of

97

having done business on that corner for—what did you tell me?—fifteen years."

"That's right." He smiled blandly at me.

"And I suppose you don't know anything about the people at the Globe Hotel, either."

He reached into his pocket for another cigarette, frowning. "Like I said, I don't have anything to do with that bunch of slopes."

"They're not all 'slopes,' Otis."

"No? Well, maybe not. I wouldn't know. I just mind my own business, look out for my theatres, and then—"

"I know, come home to your horses."

He shook out his match and paused, eyeing me for a few seconds before he tossed it into the frog's mouth. "That's exactly what I do."

"With a few stops on the way."

"What's that supposed to mean?"

"You know a young Vietnamese woman named Dolly Vang?"

"Who?"

"Dolly Vang. She lives at the Globe."

He narrowed his eyes in such a parody of thoughtfulness that I almost laughed. "Maybe I do," he said. "They all look alike—"

"You were seen in the stairwell of the hotel with Dolly earlier this week."

"Oh, that one."

"That one."

"Funny little slope. Took the name Dolly because she admires Dolly Parton. Wants to be just like her. Thought of bleaching her hair blond, but her mother wouldn't let her. I'll tell you, though, it'll take some effort in the tits department—"

"What were you doing with Dolly?"

Anger flashed across his face, but he controlled it quickly, his expression settling back into its good-old-country-boy lines. "Well, what do you think I could have been doing—in a stairwell, for Christ's sake."

"I should have asked what you were talking about."

"What do *you* think?"

Now that he'd told me about Dolly's show business fixation, it was obvious. "She wants to get into the movies."

"Right. Little Dolly wants to be a star."

"Does she know what kind of films you make?"

"Sure she does. Girl's got eyes. May not speak the language so good, but she's not stupid."

"And she still wants to get into your films?"

"Sure."

Duc Vang had been worried about his sisters' eager adoption of American names and styles; I now wondered if he also had guessed Dolly's ambitions. "What did you tell her?"

"What I'd tell any smart and willing young lady—once the production company's moved over to the Crystal Palace, we'll give her a screen test." He smiled evilly and the country-boy facade dropped away. I was looking at the real Otis Knox now, and what I saw made me a little sick.

Unwilling to let him see my reaction, I said casually, "Oh, you're moving the production company there too?"

"Yeah. Basement's honeycombed with dressing rooms; you don't need those if you're only showing films. So next week I'm getting the work crews in there, and they'll rip them out, and I'll have one hell of a good sound stage. I tell you, that Dolly was impressed when I showed her what we planned to do."

"You showed her?"

His evil grin widened. "Sure. Took her over there last Friday, when I got possession of the place. Gave her a little private screen test. That girl's going to be all right."

My fingers tightened around the beer bottle.

"Don't throw it, honey," Knox said.

"What, and waste good Stroh's?" I forced myself to take a last swallow, then set the bottle on the floor.

I was about to stand up when the phone rang. Knox excused himself and went to answer it. The instrument was straight out of the fifties—a Mickey Mouse set, where you talked into the ears. I sat there, watching one of the king-pins of San Francisco's porno racket looking like a Mouseketeer with his headpiece on crooked.

"Yeah," Knox said impatiently, "now what?" He listened for a moment, then turned so his back was to me. "Tonight?" his voice was muffled now. "Why?" There was another pause and then, "Ah, shit! All right. I'll be there as soon as I can."

When he turned to me, his face was twisted with an-noyance. "Look, honey, I've got to go."

I stood up. "Is there a problem?"

He ignored the question and came to stand close to me—too close. "I guess you didn't get what you came for, honey."

I shrugged and reached into my bag for my keys.

He moved closer. "You come back some other night, we'll take up where we left off."

I could feel his body heat, smell his unpleasant, musky aftershave. Just before he reached for me, I stepped back and looked him over slowly, allowing my gaze to linger on his thinning hair.

Knox quickly put a hand to where its wispy strands rose in blowdried waves from his widow's peak. I smiled—as evilly, I hoped, as he had earlier. Then I turned and walked out of the house.

— 13 —

When I got back to the city, I drove to the Tenderloin and parked in the same lot on Eddy Street as before. A fine rain was misting my car windows, but it hadn't begun to come down hard; I walked over to Market, where Carolyn Bui's office was, detouring a couple of blocks to take a look at the Crystal Palace Theatre. After talking to Knox, I was curious about the place.

It was a massive white structure, its facade begrimed and pitted. The marquee, which once had glittered with hundreds of colored lights, was dark, its bulbs missing or broken. There were cornices around the roofline—gargoyles and griffons and other fantastical beasts—but many had crumbled away, and scaffolding had been erected over the sidewalk to protect pedestrians. The scaffolding itself was plastered with tattered notices of lost dogs, political rallies, and countercultural events. Graffiti was spray-painted there too: GAY POWER; NO VIETNAM IN CENTRAL AMERICA; PAT LOVES WALT; DEATH TO EVERYBODY. I stared at the last, then shook my head. Eventually, of course, the graffiti artist would have his wish.

Similar black thoughts pressed down on me as I made my way along the wet sidewalk. The rain had started in earnest now, and I passed bums sheltering themselves in doorways or, in a couple of cases, under the benches that had been part of the Market Street beautification project. What few pedestrians there were hurried along, umbrellas or rainhats tilted against the downpour. Trolley buses and taxis sped by in the curb lane, tossing up waves of water. When I got to the old office building that housed the Refugee Assistance Center I rushed into the lobby, pulling off my floppy red hat and brushing at my suede jacket, which now resembled part of an old spotted cow.

A security guard at the lobby desk took my name and called upstairs, then motioned at the bank of elevators. Relieved that Carolyn was still in the office, I rode to the third floor and followed the corridor to its end. The reception room of the Center was cheerful—each wall painted a different bright color and covered with posters—and children's toys were scattered on the oval rag rug. I'd been here before during business hours and had watched the refugee children crawling around, happily at play while their parents conferred with the Center's social workers on such life-and-death matters as food, shelter, and medical care.

101

Carolyn's voice called out to me from one of the doors off the reception area, and I went over there. She sat at her desk, feet propped on a pulled-out drawer, delicate oval face drawn and weary. "I'd about given up on you," she said.

I took off my jacket and hung it over a chair to dry. "I hope you didn't stay here on my account," I said. "If you hadn't been in the office, I would have called you at home."

"No, like I said on the phone earlier, I had work to catch up on anyway."

I looked at my watch and was surprised to see it was almost nine. And then I remembered the note I'd left for Hank. "Good Lord! May I use your phone?"

She pushed it across the desk to me.

Quickly I dialed All Souls. Someone whose voice I didn't recognize answered and went away to fetch Hank. When he came on the line, he sounded as unconcerned as if I'd been off on a Sunday school picnic.

"I just wanted to tell you I'm okay," I said.

"Huh?"

"I'm okay. You don't have to notify the sheriff."

"About what?"

"I left you a note—"

"What note?"

"You didn't get it? I slipped it under your office door around four-thirty."

"Oh. I wasn't in the office then, and I haven't gone back there since."

Even though I knew it was unreasonable, I felt a little hurt and neglected. "Where the hell were you?"

"The Remedy Lounge." It was Hank's favorite sleazy bar.

"Great. I could have been getting killed because you were guzzling Scotch with a bunch of barflies."

"I don't guzzle." Hank was used to my small but dramatic fits of pique; he didn't sound alarmed, much less offended by my aspersions upon his watering hole. "Who was trying to kill you?"

"No one. Never mind. I'll check in with you tomorrow."
I replaced the receiver and glanced at Carolyn, expecting at
least a quizzical look. She was staring off into space, apparently not having heard a word of my conversation.

"Bad day?" I said gently.

She rolled her eyes and put her fingertips to her forehead. "Bad is not the word. I was closeted with our board
for hours. Do you know anything about nonprofit organizations?"

"Well, I guess I work for one, since All Souls seldom
makes a profit. But, no, not in the formal sense."

"Their boards can be ineffectual and nit-picking, to say
the least. Often the members are appointed because they're
the only ones willing to serve. Ours is particularly bad;
those people know nothing of the real world, and they can't
comprehend what we're up against."

Realizing she needed to talk it out, I said, "You're trying
to cope with some pretty bad problems, aren't you?"

"The problems are enormous. We've had an influx of
thousands of people in this city that will affect us for decades to come. How we deal with it now determines how
positive or negative their impact will be. They are people
who have no assets, who don't know the language, who
don't understand the way we live. They have to be fed,
housed, and eventually acculturated. The one thing we
have going for us is that they're ambitious and willing to
learn. They *want* to make a way for themselves. But that's
about all we've got going."

"I guess the language barrier is the biggest problem?"

"It's one of the biggest. With the educated refugees, it's
merely a matter of getting them into intensive classes; in a
short time they're ready to resume their former profes-
sions, run a business, or acquire some technical training.
But then you have others—the Hmong, for instance."

"Who?"

"The Hmong. They're a primitive Laotian tribe. 'Free
People,' the name means. They're great fighters; fought
fiercely against the Communists. The U.S. government allowed fifty-eight thousand of them to emigrate in 1978, in

recognition of their anti-Communist activities. Fortunately for me, most of them have been resettled in rural communities—there are twelve thousand of them in Fresno County alone. But you know what? The Hmong don't even have a written language."

"You're kidding."

"No, I'm not. It's difficult enough to teach English to educated Asians. But can you imagine how it is when you can't even start from such a simple basis as *writing?*"

"No, truthfully, I can't."

Carolyn sat up, facing me, gesturing in short, clipped motions. In spite of her obvious weariness, I sensed she was tightly wound. "So there's the language barrier," she went on. "Then you've got housing. Where do you *put* these people? They have no money; we don't have much either; rents in San Francisco are high. Where you put them is in the Tenderloin. If you're lucky, the building is as nice as the Globe Hotel. But you're not always lucky. I *hate* having to locate my people in the Tenderloin. It's like throwing a baby into a lions' den."

I thought of the Globe Hotel. By Tenderloin standards, it *was* nice. People there—the Caucasians like Sallie Hyde and Mary Zemanek—genuinely cared for the refugees. But the rest of the Tenderloin was not like that; it was full of people who preyed on the culturally innocent Vietnamese, people like Otis Knox . . .

Carolyn seemed to have sensed what I was thinking, because she said, "It's not just the drug pushers or the pimps. You've also got the lunatics—"

"Like Brother Harry, the street preacher."

"Yes, like Brother Harry. He's acting out what psychologists call 'grandiose behavior.' He thinks he has instructions from God to save souls, and he does it in bizarre ways, such as random preaching to crowds."

Involuntarily, I thought of Jesus Christ. *He* had preached randomly to crowds, and you certainly couldn't say those loaves and fishes weren't bizarre.

"So far," Carolyn said, "Harry's behavior has merely been strange, not dangerous. But there's always the chance it will take a turn for the worse. And there are plenty of others like him. That man in the military uniform who marches up and down the sidewalk, saluting and giving orders. The old lady with the umbrella that's just spokes. Have you seen her? She keeps it open, rain or shine. And then there's the man with the chisel who chips the mosaics off the facade of the Taj Mahal Bar on Turk Street. He chips them off, the owner eventually replaces them, and then he chips them off again."

She paused, a little calmer for saying her piece. "The newspapers are always writing features about those people. They call them 'colorful characters.' They sure are—but what happens when they cease to be merely colorful and become dangerous?"

"What indeed?" I said. "There's not a great deal that *can* be done." The police code 800 signifies "insanity in the streets," and summons officers to the scene of such incidents. However, unless a person appears to be an immediate threat to himself or to others, he cannot be detained. If he *does* seem dangerous, he can be held for observation for only seventy-two hours; most persons are released at the end of the period with only a referral to a mental health center. And few make use of the referral.

"Carolyn," I said after a moment, "do you consider Brother Harry dangerous?"

"He's a hater. But dangerous? I don't know."

"What about Jimmy Milligan?"

"Who?"

"He's a bearded man who recites poetry. Sort of elfin in appearance."

"Oh, him. I've seen him around the Globe. Mary Zemanek gives him odd jobs occasionally. Why don't you ask her?"

I had, and Mary had seemed to think highly of Jimmy. "What about the others who live at the Globe?"

"I can only speak for the people we've placed there, and they're all good citizens—or, I should say, would-be citizens. Of course, there *is* the fat woman."

"Who?"

"That flower seller who brought you up to the Vangs' apartment the other day. Sallie Hyde."

"What about her?"

"She's a murderess."

"What!"

Carolyn held up a cautioning hand. "Well, it happened a long time ago. I only know of it because her former parole officer is on our board. But Sallie Hyde spent seven years in prison for killing a child she was babysitting. You'd have to ask the parole officer—she's retired now—for particulars."

It gave me pause, and also a sense of sadness, because I liked Sallie Hyde. Still, murderers sometimes *did* repeat their crimes, if the killings grew out of some deep-rooted inner disturbance. "What's the parole officer's name?"

Carolyn opened her address book and read off the woman's name and number. Then she looked at her watch. "I'm starved. Have you eaten?"

"No," I said, realizing I'd had nothing all day but the beer with Otis Knox. Originally I'd felt too choked up because of the murder to eat; now I was famished.

"Good," Carolyn said. "Let's walk over to Lan's Garden. It's a good restaurant and I can guarantee the Vangs will provide us with a feast. Also, you'll have a captive audience for any questions you might want to ask."

Lan's Garden was small, with about ten tables constructed of a natural blond wood. A single carnation in a chunky glass vase sat on each table, and the walls were covered with grass mats. Airline posters tacked at regular intervals depicted scenes of Southeast Asia.

Lan Vang stood behind the cash-register counter next to the door, adding up a stack of guest checks. Although she looked tired, she wore a royal blue dress that complemented her pale complexion in a way that made me realize how pretty she was. When she saw Carolyn and me, her expression brightened and she ushered us to a table with great ceremony. Then she went through the swinging doors at the back of the restaurant, clapping her hands together and calling out in Vietnamese.

Although it was late, there were several parties at other tables, all of them Orientals. I said to Carolyn, "This looks like a popular place."

"When you taste the food, you'll know why."

"How long have the Vangs been in business?"

"About three years. When they came to this country, they got started by going out and getting jobs—all of them except the little ones, full-time, part-time, anything anybody would let them do. Then when they had a little capital, they borrowed from their friends, in the Asian way, with no interest and no payback date. The restaurant is now turning a profit, and most of those loans have been repaid."

Lan returned with a pot of tea, two cups, and menus. When she had gone back to the kitchen, Carolyn continued, "Of course, the Vangs have been lucky. This is a good location, on a well-lighted corner, and the landlord doesn't seem interested in raising the rent. That's been a problem for many businesses here—their success hampers them."

"How so?"

"Normally Tenderloin commercial space is considered so undesirable that it doesn't even rent by the square foot. Our people are able to get their business places cheap—for instance, the Vangs pay only three hundred and seventy-five dollars a month for this restaurant. But then they fix the places up and start turning a profit, and the landlords realize their property is worth something after all. So they either raise the rent or evict the tenants who did the fixing up, in order to rent to someone who can afford to pay a great deal more."

"Aren't there laws against that?"

"You're thinking of rent control; that doesn't apply to commercial property."

"Well, can't something be done about it?"

Again Carolyn looked weary. "In a small way. One of our sister organizations, the Center for Southeast Asian

Resettlement, has bought a fourteen-thousand-square-foot building on O'Farrell Street as its headquarters, as well as for medical services, community space, and refugee shops. That will keep rents stable for the few businesses they can accommodate. It's a drop in the bucket, but I'm hoping someday we'll be able to do something similar, and then maybe other groups will follow suit. Until then . . ."

One of the Vang daughters—Susan—came up to the table, order pad in hand. I reached for the menu, but Carolyn waved my hand away. "Let me order." She spoke rapidly in Vietnamese, and Susan smiled and scribbled on the pad. As she was about to go back to the kitchen, I said, "Susan, is Dolly here tonight?"

"No. She has a test in her class tomorrow and went home early to study."

I thought of the other "test" Dolly had taken recently. "What is she studying?"

"Shorthand, at the business college. She wishes to become a secretary."

Obviously Dolly was keeping her real ambitions to herself. "What about Duc? Is he working tonight?"

"No, not Duc either. The sadness over his friend's death is still very much with him, and our father decided he should have some time to himself."

I nodded, and Susan left for the kitchen.

"Why are you so interested in Dolly and Duc?" Carolyn asked.

"Duc is an interesting person. We had a good talk earlier today, and I'd like to continue it."

"And Dolly?"

Briefly I debated telling Carolyn about Otis Knox, but then decided against it. She had had a bad day, and I didn't want to burden her further. "Same reason."

Carolyn looked unbelieving, but didn't press the issue. Instead we talked about the problems she had when relocating her clients in Tenderloin hotels—drug dealing and thefts from the rooms; the repetitious police narcotics raids; overdoses and knifings in the hallways; the caches of stolen goods and illegal weapons.

Then our food came: there was chicken flavored with five mysterious spices, beef with something called lemon grass, and mint-flavored shrimp and pork in delicate rice skins. All of it was wonderful, and we ate ravenously, in total silence. When we were finished, Lan emerged from the kitchen carrying another pot of tea and two more cups. With her was a stocky man whom she introduced as her husband, Chinh. The other customers had left by then, so Lan and Chinh sat down to relax with us, Lan removing her shoes and wiggling her toes luxuriously.

At first we talked of inconsequential matters: the earlier downpour, which had now subsided; Christmas, and how much shopping we had left to do; the new tree that had mysteriously appeared in the Globe lobby. I was interested to learn that Christmas was not a holiday the Vangs had adopted upon coming to the United States; they, and many of their friends, were Catholic and had celebrated it all their lives. Finally the conversation turned to more serious affairs: the Dinh boy's death, and their son Duc's deep grief.

"He seems to blame himself," Lan said, "and the sorrow grows, rather than diminishes."

"He is so serious," Chinh added, "so unlike our other children."

I said, "He seems very concerned with the traditional Vietnamese values."

"Too much so," his father replied. "We respect the old ways, of course. But we are making a life in a new country now, and we must try—"

The door behind us burst open, and we all turned. Dolly Vang stood there, her mouth open, one hand clawing at the ends of a scarf she had tied over her hair. Her eyes were like black holes in her ashen face. She stood there, seemingly unable to speak, looking wildly from one to the other of us.

Lan rose and spoke to her in their native language.

Dolly just stood there, clutching at the scarf.

I got up and went over to her. "Dolly, what's wrong?" She looked imploringly at me. Whatever had upset her

109

seemed to have driven both her English and her Vietnamese from her head. Finally she drew in a gasping breath and said, "You must help."

"Help with what? What's happened?"

"Please." She grasped my arm above my elbow, her fingers digging into my flesh.

The others rose and started toward us. I held up my hand. "Let me handle this."

They looked at me and then at one another, doubt and concern plain on their faces.

Dolly tugged at me. "Please!"

"Stay here," I said to Carolyn. "Keep everyone here. I'll phone you when I know what the trouble is."

Then Dolly was pulling me from the restaurant, her grip on my arm so tight it hurt. "Please," she said again, "we must hurry!"

— 14 —

Dolly led me down the street at a fast pace, clutching my hand now. Her English seemed to have deserted her once more, and we rushed past the bars and greasy spoons and cheap hotels in silence. Her breath came in ragged gasps, and her small fingers grasped mine like a cold metal trap. Twice I glanced back to see if anyone from Lan's Garden was following us, but if they had, they'd fallen far behind.

The rain had stopped, leaving a mist that blunted the sharpness of the neon signs and masked the ugliness of the buildings they adorned. The temperature was warmer, the air washed fresh, and the night people had emerged from whatever shelter they had taken. Dolly weaved expertly among them, oblivious to the lewd and enticing comments some of the men yelled at us.

After we had rounded a couple of corners, I realized she was not taking me to the Globe Hotel, as I'd originally supposed. Instead, she seemed to be angling toward Market Street. We passed down a particularly dark block with a row of burnt-out and boarded-up buildings, and I glanced warily into their shadows. Dolly, however, did not seem aware of our surroundings.

The muted amber streetlights that lined Market were visible ahead of us. Half a block from the corner, Dolly stopped abruptly and let go of my hand. I looked around and realized we were on the side street next to the Crystal Palace Theatre. The scaffolding extended along this side of the building also, and there was a black Ford Bronco parked under its overhang. Otis Knox owned a black Bronco; I'd seen it only hours before, parked between the golden arches at his ranch. Had he come into the city after I'd left him? Was that what the phone call he'd gotten had been about? Perhaps it had been from Dolly . . .

I turned to her and saw she was staring at a backlit opening in the scaffolding, twisting the ends of her scarf. "What now?" I finally said. In spite of the traffic sounds from the surrounding streets, it was quiet here, and my voice sounded unusually loud.

She turned her face toward me, black eyes gleaming against its pale oval. "Come, please," she said and started forward on tiptoe, toward the opening.

I followed, hand poised over the pocket in my bag where my .38 rested. Knox was here, and he had probably done something to frighten Dolly—perhaps to hurt her. I would not have gone in there unarmed.

The opening in the scaffolding led to a narrow walkway next to the wall of the theatre. The light I had seen came from bare bulbs that had been strung at intervals, probably as a security precaution. I followed Dolly's slender back, steadying myself with one hand on the rain-damp wall, so I wouldn't stumble on the broken glass and other scattered debris. Dolly moved toward where the building fronted on Market Street and finally stopped at a side exit door that stood partway open. She turned to me and motioned wordlessly at the door.

Suddenly I wondered if this was a trap—some plot Otis Knox had concocted to get even with me for my earlier putdown and then had enlisted Dolly to help him carry out. I said, "All right, Dolly, we're here. Now tell me what's going on."

"Please," she said, "you must help me." The words came out in an anguished whisper, and I knew she was not playing a game. Something terrible had happened to Dolly inside this theatre . . .

I reached into my bag for the small flashlight I carry there and handed it to her. "You take this and lead me." Then I got out my gun and released the safety catch. At the sound, Dolly whirled. Her eyes went to the gun, and she froze.

Of course Dolly had had plenty of bad experience with guns in Vietnam. Quickly I said, "It's all right. It's to protect us." Then I gave her a gentle shove, and she started through the exit door as if she were sleepwalking.

The door opened into the lobby. What light there was came from the plate-glass entry at the front of the theatre. Directly ahead on the far side was a wide marble stairway that probably led up to the balcony; to the left was an empty candy counter, popcorn and soft-drink machines still in place. On either side of the counter were large swinging doors that led to the main part of the theatre.

Dolly had stopped again and was holding the flashlight limply, so it shone on the floor, picking out a gold fleur-de-lis pattern on the worn blue carpet. I took hold of her hand and positioned it so the flash shone straight ahead of us. The beam wavered as tremors shook her small body.

I waited, listening, and heard nothing but distant street sounds. Leaning closer to Dolly, I whispered, "Now where?" She started forward, in that same sleepwalking gait, and led me into the main part of the theatre.

The shaky beam of the flash showed rows upon rows of seats upholstered in worn blue velvet. The side walls had

112

gold-railed boxes projecting from them, their entrances draped in the same material as the seats. The stage curtains carried out the fleur-de-lis pattern of the carpet. It smelled stale and closed-up in there, and the air was colder than outside on the street. Beside me, Dolly began to tremble harder, and she jerked the flashlight. Its beam darted toward the vaulted ceiling, revealing a huge crystal-and-gilt chandelier.

Dolly got the flashlight under control and began to walk down the aisle toward the stage. I followed, holding my gun. There was no sound but the brushing of our footsteps on the carpet. We mounted the stage on the left side, and Dolly pulled the curtains apart and motioned for me to pass through. I looked around them cautiously, breathing in their musty odor. There was no one, nothing, on the stage.

When I turned to her, Dolly was hanging back on the other side of the curtain. I gestured for her to come ahead. She did so, walking with more determination now and holding the light steady on the second set of curtains at the rear of the stage. We crossed the great empty space—our footsteps echoing hollowly now—and moved into the darkness beyond.

At first I could make out only abstract shapes. Then I saw that they were ropes and metal scaffolding and ladders that rose up toward the catwalks and lighting grid overhead. At the extreme back were bulky objects, probably stored scenery flats.

Dolly was shining the flash at the floor once more, and I turned to her in exasperation. I was about to speak sharply to her when I looked along its beam, downward and to the left. Near the base of one of the ladders.

A man lay crumpled there. A man in cowboy boots, jeans, and a western shirt. Otis Knox.

I jammed the gun into my bag, grabbed the flashlight from Dolly, and went over to him. He lay on his side, legs splayed, one arm outflung, the other bent under him. His head was cocked back at an odd angle, and streaks of blood spread out from under it.

113

Knowing it was hopeless, I tried to find a pulse. Nothing. His flesh was pliant and beginning to cool. His neck was undoubtedly broken.

This was too much. Two people dead, in two days. Two times, kneeling next to a body . . .

And then I had a jarring thought: Dolly had killed him. She had killed him and now she wanted me to cover it up.

I felt a familiar reflex—the sudden intake of breath that would quickly turn into uncontrollable gasps. I told myself I couldn't give in to it; I had to deal with this situation, deal with Dolly. And as I shuddered with the first gasp, I felt her come up behind me, shaking as badly as I was.

Weakly I stood and put my arm around her, telling myself I would have to control my breathing. And, miraculously, I felt it return to normal. I waited, holding Dolly tighter, but there were no more spasms in my diaphragm.

Good Lord, I thought, maybe I've just learned something. Something about the power of my own will. Maybe I've discovered some strength I never knew I had.

I moved Dolly back, away from Knox's body, and shone the flashlight over it and then up the ladder at the lighting grid above. There was a narrow catwalk that led over to the ladder on the other side of this space; other catwalks branched off from it over the stage. Had he fallen from up there? It seemed likely. But what had he been doing up there in the first place?

When I lowered the light and held it so it illuminated where Dolly and I stood, I saw she was crying. Huge tears flowed unchecked down her cheeks, but she made no sound. Gently I said, "When did you find him?"

She paused a moment, fighting for control. "It was just before I came to the restaurant for help. I saw his car. I came inside. I found him." Seeing Knox's body this second time apparently had unleashed her powers of speech. I remained silent, letting her tell it, trying to gauge her truthfulness.

"I came in, but he was not downstairs where we always go . . ." And then she stopped, putting her hands to her

114

face. She scrubbed at the tears, looked up again. "I am so ashamed."

"You don't need to explain. I know."

"You . . . *know?*"

"Yes. Knox told me."

"He told you." Her voice was flat, dead.

"Don't be ashamed, Dolly. Just go on and tell me what happened."

In the same flat tone, she said, "I looked for him downstairs. He was not there. I called out. He did not answer. Then I came up here, and I found him."

"How did you see him? Did you have a flashlight?"

She looked down at her empty right hand. "I must have. I do not remember . . ."

I shone my own flash around at the floor. There was another, several feet from Knox's body, and it tended to substantiate Dolly's story. "You must have dropped it. Where did you get it in the first place?"

"Downstairs? Yes, now I remember. Downstairs, where the movies are to be made."

"Were the lights on down there?"

"Yes."

Knox must have had PG&E turn on the power; or perhaps it had been on all along. "But none were on up here?"

"No."

"All right. Did you come in here just because you saw Knox's car—or did you have an appointment with him?"

"No, I had no appointment. I was walking home, but the rain had stopped, and I wanted to walk a little more. So I came down here, to look at the theatre where I would become a film star. He"—she motioned in the direction of the body—"was going to make me a film star. Here, in this theatre."

You bet he was, I thought.

"He said he loved me. I would be famous. He told me I was beautiful. No one had ever said that before." She paused, then added, "But he also told you about . . . us."

A wonderful thing had happened in Dolly Vang's life. Or

115

at least she had thought so. It was probably the only wonderful thing in a life of hardship, and now it was not only taken away, but tarnished. Still, I said nothing to soften the blow; its pain would shield her from future mistakes.

Part of me still couldn't shake the suspicion that she might have killed Knox. I said, "So you came inside. You went downstairs, looked for Knox, got the flashlight, and came up here."

"Yes. He was . . . ." She put her hands to her face and began the strange, soundless crying again.

"Stop it, Dolly," I said, more harshly than I'd intended. I realized I was angry: at Dolly, for letting herself be taken in by the likes of Otis Knox; at Knox, for using her need for attention to his own advantage; at Knox's killer—be it Dolly herself or someone else—for taking his life. Whatever else he had been, Otis Knox had also been a human being, with dreams and enthusiasms and hopes like all the rest of us. No one, for whatever reason, had the right to end that life.

Dolly was looking at me with wide, hurt eyes. I didn't apologize for my sharpness. "Why didn't you go for the police?" I asked.

"I . . ."

"Why didn't you go out and stop one of the beat officers? Or flag down a patrol car? There are plenty around. Why go to the restaurant?"

"I . . . I did not wish anyone to know I had been here."

"But you would have had to tell your family, if I hadn't been there. You would have had to bring someone here—your father or perhaps your brother Duc."

"Yes, but they are family. If anyone must know, it is them. But I did not wish an outsider to know my shame."

"Then why bring me here?"

She paused. "I do not know. In some way, I do not feel you are an outsider. I could tell you cared about us, when you came that first day. And you are a woman; I guess I thought you would understand."

I wondered if her pretty little speech was designed to further enlist my sympathies. And then I felt ashamed too—but for vastly different reasons than Dolly. I hated it when I went all cynical and suspicious and cold. It happened more and more often, the longer I stayed in this business. But that didn't mean I had to like it.

I put my arm around Dolly once more and said, "Well, I'm afraid the police are going to have to know. We've got to tell them right away." I started to lead her toward the curtains and the stage beyond, but she hung back, head turned toward the body. Tremors began to pass through her slight frame again.

"Don't, Dolly," I said softly. "Let's just go."

"But to leave him again. . . . It is so dark here."

Yes, it was dark there—and also wherever Otis Knox was now. "Come on, Dolly," I said. "There's nothing you can do for him anymore."

— 15 —

When I found a phone booth I dialed SFPD Homicide and asked for Greg Marcus. He was still at the Hall, and his presence at this late hour probably meant that another case was breaking, or just beginning. For a moment he sounded as if he might turn Knox's death over to someone else—exactly what I didn't want. While Greg and I would always be separated by the barrier that comes from being former lovers, he was a good cop and I hoped he'd listen to the fragments of an idea that I was beginning to gather.

While I spoke with Greg, Dolly stood outside the booth, one hand on the glass of the door, as if she was afraid she might lose touch with me. She stared down the misty, amber-lighted expanse of Market Street toward the theatre where Knox's body lay. Dolly was another reason I wanted

Greg on the scene; in addition to being a good cop, he was a gentle man, and he would deal far better with this frightened girl than would most of the other men on the squad.

Greg put me on hold for a few seconds, then came back on the line and said a squad car was on its way to the theatre; he would meet us there as soon as he could, and we should do nothing until he arrived. I hung up the receiver and opened the door. "Dolly, what's the phone number at your family's restaurant?"

"At . . . No, you must not tell my parents—"

"I only want to say that we're all right."

She hesitated, then said, "The number is 525-9177."

"Thank you." I dialed, and the phone was answered immediately by Lan Vang, her voice high-pitched with anxiety. Without elaboration, I told her we were in no trouble and would return to the hotel within the hour. Then I asked to speak with Carolyn. To her, I explained a little more—that a friend of Dolly's had been killed in an accident and we were waiting for the police. I asked if Carolyn would go back to the Globe with the Vangs and stay until we arrived. In spite of what I knew must by now be boneweariness, Carolyn agreed without hesitation.

When I stepped out of the booth, Dolly turned to me, wide eyes searching my face. "It's all right," I said. "I didn't tell them any more than I had to." I paused, then added, "Of course you'll have to explain everything. They'll need to know."

She looked away, toward a darkened and barred storefront. I touched her shoulder and motioned toward the theatre. We started down the near-deserted sidewalk. An occasional cab cruised slowly by to see if we were potential fares; the few trolley buses that passed were almost empty of passengers. I looked at my watch and saw it was well after midnight. Halfway to the theatre, we began to hear a siren, and Dolly moved closer to me and slipped her small hand into mine. She had stopped trembling, but her fingers were icy and she didn't speak.

The uniformed men were getting out of the cruiser when

we got there, hands poised above their guns. The squad car's headlights bathed the rough wooden scaffolding, and the beams of the flashing blue and red beacons bounced off the graffiti and notices posted there. I identified myself and told them Lt. Marcus had asked us not do anything until he arrived. They looked dubious about that, but left us alone until Greg pulled up a few minutes later in an unmarked car. As he came toward us, Dolly shrank against me, and I said, "It's all right; he's a friend." To Greg, I said, "Thanks for coming," realizing the tea-party words sounded ridiculous.

One corner of his mouth twitched, and I knew he'd also recognized the absurdity. He looked tired and unusually grim. "Sure. I was just interrogating a Forest Hills mother of two who decided to take an axe to the family tonight. Frankly, I was glad to turn it over to one of the inspectors; I don't have the stomach for some things that I used to. Now, what's happened here?"

I explained, from the beginning. When I got to the part about Dolly and Otis Knox being "friends," Greg's eyes flicked to her, then back to me, and the knowledge in them told me I wouldn't have to spell it out. When I finished, he merely said, "Okay, show me where the body is."

We showed him, Dolly sticking to me like a little burr, and then the lab men took over. The patrolmen had located a lighting panel in one of the wings, and the stage was now brightly lit. Dolly and I stood to one side, silent while Greg conferred with the technicians and an inspector named Mourant, who had shown up right behind them. When he finally rejoined us, I said, "Would it be possible for us to go back to the hotel? Dolly's had a rough time, and her parents are bound to be worried about her. You could question her at her apartment, and there's a woman there who can interpret, if necessary."

"That's not a bad idea, but let me talk with you for a minute." He put his hand on my elbow and led me a few paces away. "This looks to be a simple case of accidental death," he said in a lower voice, "but there's something in

119

your manner that hints otherwise. Do you think the girl was responsible?"

"Initially I suspected something of the sort, but not anymore. Can't we go into this later?"

"Go into it now."

I fought down my annoyance at the order, reminding myself that it belonged to another time, when I had had a right to take offense. "I was at Otis Knox's ranch in Marin County earlier tonight."

Greg's eyebrows shot up.

"In connection with the Globe Hotel business," I added hastily. "When I first talked with Knox—to get a feel for the neighborhood—he claimed he knew nothing about the hotel or what he referred to as 'a bunch of slopes.' But then I heard about his connection with Dolly and decided to drive out to Nicasio and question him. When I arrived, Knox looked settled in for the night, but as I was starting to leave, he had a phone call. I suspect he planned to come back to the city."

"Any idea who the call was from?"

"No, but I think I can reconstruct what he said. And he seemed . . . well, not upset, but as if he didn't like whatever the caller wanted."

"I see. We'll discuss it in more detail later. But now, because I know you—and you must admit I know you well— let me tell you what I sense is going on in your head."

I braced myself, already aware—because I also knew *him* well—of what was to follow.

"You think," he said, "that phone call was a lure. You think someone wanted to kill Knox, so he phoned him, enticed him to this theatre, and murdered him."

"It's possible."

"Some clever killer. While he was enticing him to the theatre, he decided he might just as well entice him up onto a catwalk above the stage. And then he climbed up there after him—this, mind you, without making our Mr. Knox the least bit suspicious—and pushed him to his death. Is that how you see it?"

120

"Greg . . ." But put in those terms, it *did* seem silly.

"And you also think, because of the connection with the Vang girl, that Knox's death might have something to do with the killing at the Globe Hotel."

I had considered the possibility, but now I was damned if I would admit it.

"In a neighborhood where there are random murders every day," Greg went on, "you want to connect these particular deaths, because the Vang girl knew both victims."

Dammit, *why* had I wanted Greg on the scene? Had time—plus his good behavior the night before—made me forget how sarcastic and cutting he could be? What an idiot I'd been to think he would listen to me! Especially to an idea that was only half-formed—worse than that, not an idea at all but more a feeling that everything here was not as it looked on the surface.

But I'd been right about those kinds of feelings before. And Greg knew that. I glared up at him, not speaking.

"All right," he finally said, "take the Vang girl back to the hotel. But don't talk to anyone outside; there's a crowd, and I don't know if any of them are from the media, but if they are, I don't want them getting wind of who the victim is yet."

He wasn't going to argue with me; he wasn't going to try to poke any more holes in what remained of my reasoning. And that meant something. It meant he was remembering those other times I'd been right.

I went over to Dolly and took her arm. "Come on," I said, "I'll take you home."

When we got back to the hotel, the small lobby was jammed with people, most of them Vietnamese. Given the presence of the little Christmas tree, it could have been a festive holiday gathering—except for the anxious expressions on the participants' faces. They milled about, talking in low voices, and as we entered, Lan Vang threw herself upon her daughter, as if to shelter her from further harm.

For a moment I felt a stab of alarm. Had something else

121

happened here at the hotel while Dolly and I had been dealing with the police at the theatre? But then I caught a glimpse of Carolyn and Mary Zemanek over by the door to the manager's apartment. Neither of them looked particularly upset, so I chalked up the others' agitation to worry over Dolly.

Lan Vang clasped my hand and said, "Thank you. Thank you for taking care of my daughter."

I looked at Dolly. She had been leaning on her mother, but now she pulled herself erect, and I suspected she was thinking about the explanations ahead. I said, "I was glad to help, Lan. Why don't you take Dolly upstairs now, away from this crowd? She's had a bad time."

Lan nodded and tugged at her daughter. Dolly hesitated, then followed her toward the elevator, looking back with pleading eyes. I shook my head at her. This was Dolly's problem.

With the departure of the Vangs, the lobby began to empty and soon only Mary Zemanek, Carolyn, and I remained. Carolyn crossed to me and said, "Now will you please explain what has happened? I've been going crazy, trying to figure it out."

"I told you on the phone—"

"No, I want the full story."

I glanced at Mary. She was standing next to the Christmas tree, obviously with no intention of leaving.

"Later," I said to Carolyn.

"Miss McCone," Mary said, "I think I deserve an explanation too. What happens to the residents of this hotel—"

"It's none of your business." The words popped out before I could temper my irritation.

Mary drew herself up taller—which must have been all of four-foot-eleven. In her red chenille wrapper, white hair in its net, she looked like Mrs. Santa Claus finding her husband coming in drunk on Christmas Eve.

"I'm sorry," I said quickly. "I didn't mean to snap at you, but it's police business and I can't discuss it."

"The owner—"

If I heard her invoke the powers of Roy LaFond one more time, I would run screaming into the street. Instead I grabbed Carolyn's arm and hurried her toward the front door. "Let's wait for the police outside."

The night was still clear—almost cloudless, if you looked up beyond the shabby buildings to the sky. People still prowled the streets: hookers and johns, pimps and winos, the restless and the homeless. The air had lost the freshness the earlier storm had lent it, and the characteristic stench of the Tenderloin rose around us. Carolyn leaned back against the grimy facade of the hotel, folded her arms, and waited.

I looked down the street and spotted the now-familiar figure of Jimmy Milligan shambling along, talking to himself.

"That's the fellow I mentioned earlier," I said, "the one who quotes the poetry."

"I know who he is. You're avoiding the issue."

I was, and I didn't know why. There was no reason Carolyn shouldn't know about Dolly and Otis Knox. It would upset her, because part of her job was to keep her clients from being victimized, but her feelings would be based on professional, rather than personal, considerations. No, the reason I didn't want to talk about it had to do with me, with my weariness, with my pity for Dolly.

I started to speak, but Jimmy Milligan approached us, waving, his face alive with a manic delight. When he came up, he said, "'A bloody and a sudden end . . . gunshot or a noose . . . for Death who takes what man would keep . . . leaves what man would lose.'"

"What?" I said, startled. I knew it was only more William Butler Yeats, but his choice of verse was eerily consistent with my thoughts.

"'John Kinsella's Lament for Mrs. Mary Moore.'" He waggled his head energetically. "'What shall I do for pretty girls . . . now my old bawd is dead?'"

"Jimmy," I said, "You must have memorized every word Yeats ever wrote."

"That I have, miss. Every word."

"Where did you study his work, Jimmy?"

Another violent head waggle. "Oh, here, there, everywhere."

He was clearly at the apex of his manic stage, soaring out of control. I glanced at Carolyn, who was watching him intently, as if cataloging his symptoms.

I said, "Are you a poet yourself, Jimmy?"

His elfin features crumpled, as if under a sudden weight. "Oh, I was, miss. But not for a long time now."

"But you did write poems?"

"Oh, yes, miss. Many poems. And once I had one that appeared in a magazine. A little magazine, but it was a published poem nevertheless."

I was about to ask him to recite his poem when Greg's unmarked car pulled up to the curb and he got out. He crossed the sidewalk and glanced at Jimmy, his lips twitching in irritation. Then he said to me, "All right, let's get on with this," and pushed past us into the lobby.

— 16 —

Greg had just finished questioning Dolly when all the lights went out.

We'd been sitting in the Vangs' living room, with only Dolly and her parents present. Dolly had told her story in halting English, with Carolyn assisting her occasionally, and Lan and Chinh, while obviously ashamed at airing such a matter to outsiders, had supported her in a way that made me respect them all the more.

And now the power had failed. Lan gasped and then everyone was silent. After a few seconds, Greg said, "What's with the electricity?"

I said, "It's happened frequently; it's one of the things I was hired to investigate."

"Why didn't they just call PG and E?" There was an edginess in Greg's voice that amused me; he could walk confidently into the goriest murder scene, but being in a room that had been plunged into darkness had unnerved him.

"PG and E came out," I said. "They determined that someone is shutting off the power at the main switch."

"Then why doesn't someone turn it back on? Hal," he added to Inspector Mourant, who had arrived at the hotel a short time before, "will you go down to the manager's apartment and ask her to do something about this?"

"Right, Lieutenant." I could hear Mourant bang into a table as he made his way to the door.

"You'll have to take the stairs," Carolyn said. "The elevator doesn't function during the blackouts."

Mourant muttered something that sounded like "terrific" and left the apartment.

Greg said, "Well, this is an odd way to end an interview, but I thank you for your cooperation, Ms. Vang. I'll have a statement ready for you to sign at the Hall of Justice by noon today." Then I felt his hand on my arm. "Sharon, I think we'd better let these people get some rest."

"We're leaving now, when we can't even see where we're going?"

"Yes. Give me your flashlight." The tone of his voice said that he didn't want to hear any arguments; I guessed he was feeling claustrophobic.

At the word "flashlight," Lan, who was sitting on the other side of me, made a little exclamation. She got up and rummaged in a drawer, returning moments later with a lighted candle. Its flicker illuminated a circle of tense faces—faces that quickly relaxed.

I handed Greg my flash and looked at Carolyn. "Are you coming?"

"No, I think I'll spend the night here on the couch, if no one minds."

I told her I'd be in touch, and Greg and I went out into the hallway. As we passed Sallie Hyde's door, the fat woman stuck her head out. In the flashlight's beam I could see that her hair was in big pink curlers and she wore a quilted pink housecoat. When she saw Greg and me she said, "Oh, Sharon, it's you," and regarded him with frank curiosity.

"We're just leaving," I said. "Someone's gone to throw the switch, and the lights should be on in a few minutes."

Sallie shook her head. "First Hoa Dinh. Then poor Dolly, finding that Knox swine. Now this. And to think I told everybody there was nothing to be afraid of." Quickly she withdrew into her apartment.

Greg said, "Who was that?"

"Sallie Hyde. She's a murderess."

"What?"

"Convicted, imprisoned, and paroled. She killed a child she was babysitting. It was a long time ago, and apparently she's gone straight ever since. That's all I know."

"It probably has no bearing on what's going on here, but what did you say her name was?"

"Sallie Hyde." That meant Greg would run a check on her—and I would be sure to get the information from him.

We started down the stairs, Greg holding the flashlight so it illuminated the metal tread, our footsteps echoing loudly in the empty stairwell. When we reached the second floor, the lights came back on. "Mourant must have found the switch," Greg said. To confirm his statement, when we got to the first floor, the inspector and Mary Zemanek emerged from the basement. Mary was babbling about the owner and his liability insurance, and when Greg stopped to talk to them, I went on through the lobby. Greg caught up with me on the sidewalk in front of the hotel.

"Mourant didn't see anyone down there in the basement," he said, "but he'll stay around a while in case someone tries to pull the switch again."

"Good." I turned in the direction of the lot where my MG was.

"Wait," Greg said. "I'll walk you to your car."

"It's okay. Don't trouble yourself."

"No, I want to."

With a sense of *déja vû*, I let him accompany me to the parking lot, but when we arrived all was not as it had been the night before; the chain-link fence was locked, the lot deserted. Beyond it, the MG sat waiting forlornly.

"Dammit," I said, "I should have known they'd have closed the lot by now."

"It's good I came down here with you," Greg said. "I'll drive you home, and you can pick up your car in the morning."

"I guess I have no choice."

"Gracious, aren't you?"

"Sorry. I'm just tired." To prove I had meant no offense, I took his arm companionably as we went back to where he had parked in front of the hotel.

Out of habit, Greg drove toward my old apartment building on Guerrero Street. When I realized where he was going I corrected him, giving him directions to my house on Church Street. The street was lined with cars, and one of my neighbors had parked in my driveway, as I'd told him to do when he couldn't find a space. All the lights in the nearby houses were out, the respectable working-class folks having been in bed for hours. I wanted to go to bed too— right away, and sleep for days—but Greg seemed to have no intention of leaving. He accompanied me onto the front porch and looked expectantly inside when I opened the door. Shrugging, I said, "Do you want to come in for a drink?"

"I'd like that."

I led him inside and down the tiny hall to the living room. The house had a close, shut-up feeling, and Watney didn't even come to greet me. Probably the ferocious creature had availed himself of the new cat door Don and I had installed and was out hunting mice—or dogs and small children.

Thinking of Don made me realize I hadn't spoken to him all day, not since he'd cooked the breakfast I hadn't been able to eat. I went over and pressed the playback button of my answering machine—a new acquisition, since my ser-

127

vice had recently gone bankrupt—but there was only one message, an unintelligible one from Barry the contractor, who sounded drunk. I frowned, wondering why Don hadn't called, then turned to Greg. He was looking around the room with obvious curiosity.

"All I have is red wine," I said, "and I have to warn you—it's of dubious quality."

"At three-thirty in the morning, I don't much care about quality."

"Me neither." I went into the kitchen and took down two glasses, then detoured into the bathroom. The surgical tools lay on the floor, and there were nails scattered around the shower drain. Barry's delicate operation was going slowly. I sighed, realizing I would have to go next door to the Curleys' for my morning shower; they'd been awfully understanding about helping me out—and rightfully so, after they'd recommended Barry—but this couldn't go on indefinitely. . . .

When I returned to the living room with the wine, Greg was examining the little picture of the country inn Don had bought me. I set the glasses and the bottle on the coffee table, thinking how seldom Don and I used this room. We preferred to sit at the kitchen table, but somehow Greg would have seemed out of place there. I poured wine, he came to sit beside me, and we toasted one another.

"To your new house," he said. "It's a nice place."

"Thank you. I'm quite happy with it."

"No plans to take on a roommate—your boyfriend, I mean?"

"Not at the moment. We both like our privacy and, besides, his baby grand piano wouldn't fit."

"Oh, yes—he's a musician as well as a disc jockey."

"Yes."

We fell silent, sipping wine. The silence lengthened. It wasn't a comfortable one. Finally Greg said, "Tell me about the problems at the Globe Hotel."

As I'd figured out earlier, he was taking at least some of my ideas seriously. "I outlined them to you last night."

"I'd like some more detail."

"The case has a lot of odd elements. There's the owner, who would like to unload the place, but can't do so without first evicting the tenants. Initially I thought he might be trying to scare them away, but he turns out to be a letter-of-the-law guy who's deathly afraid someone will slip on the stairs and sue him."

"And the manager, Mrs. Zemanek?"

"She's sympathetic to the tenants, but afraid of losing her job, so she backs the owner in everything."

"From the way she was talking tonight, the owner is practically sitting at the right hand of God."

"Practically. Then we have Sallie Hyde, the murderess."

"Yes, I'll check her out."

"And then there are the Vangs and the Dinhs and the other Vietnamese residents. They all seem to be hardworking, honest people. The Vangs' son Duc is a little strange—alienated, clings to the traditional ways. He and the first victim, Hoa Dinh, were best friends, and originally I thought Hoa's death might be gang related. But I talked with Inspector Loo of the Gang Task Force, as well as with Duc and other people in the neighborhood. Whatever those boys are, they're not gang members."

Greg watched me over the rim of his glass. "But something bothers you about them. Or about Duc, anyway."

"Yes. I can't put my finger on it, except that Duc was very evasive about what he and his friends do in the neighborhood. Maybe I'll talk with him again."

Greg was silent.

"What? You don't want me pursuing this?"

"It may not be to the Department's advantage."

"Greg, I've cooperated—"

"We'll talk about it tomorrow."

"But—"

"Tomorrow."

I knew that tone, so I dropped it. "Okay. Anyway, that's the cast of characters at the hotel. Then there are the outsiders: the man who I was talking with when you arrived

129

tonight; he's a little unbalanced, recites poetry all the time. There's a street preacher who has a potential streak of violence. And, of course, there's the deceased, Otis Knox."

"This preacher—he have any connection with that hotel?"

"None that I can uncover. But he did with Knox; he preaches in front of his theatre."

"What else?"

I could have mentioned the umbrella lady or the man who chipped the tiles off the Taj Mahal Bar or even Knox's young, spaced-out film projectionist, but it all seemed irrelevant, and suddenly I felt tired. "That's about it." As I spoke, my spirits dipped even lower. I'd been on the case for two days, and that was all I had to show for it—that, and two bodies in the morgue. And a power failure . . .

I frowned.

"What now?" Greg said.

"That power failure bothers me. Why tonight? At that particular time?"

"Why not?"

"Because it was late, and there were very few tenants of that hotel who were likely to be inconvenienced. They wouldn't be using their lights or the elevator . . ."

Greg shrugged, clearly uninterested, and sipped wine. Again we fell silent, and again the silence lengthened. When I glanced over at him, he was regarding me speculatively. With a shock I realized he was considering kissing me.

When the shock faded, I actually considered encouraging him. After all, Greg was an attractive man, and even at our worst times the physical part of our relationship had never cooled off. Then I thought of Don and set my wineglass on the table.

"It's awfully late," I said, "and we've both got to be at work in the morning."

Greg looked at me for a moment longer. Then he nodded and drained his glass, his face expressionless. "Thanks for the wine," he said, standing up. "Call me sometime after noon and we'll talk about you investigating further."

I followed him to the door and out into the crisp night. Here, miles from the stink of the Tenderloin, the air had a fresh quality that I could savor. For a moment, standing there on the porch, I looked up at Greg and again felt the tug of physical attraction. Apparently he felt it too, because he hesitated before he went down the steps to his car, raising a hand in farewell.

I went back inside, took the bottle and glasses to the kitchen, and turned off the lights. After groping my way to the bedroom in the dark, I shed my clothes and crawled into bed.

Only someone else was already in it. A familiar, warm, muscular body.

I hadn't seen his car; where was it? Parked far down the congested street, no doubt.

Don said, "It's about time. For a while there, I thought the three of us were going to end up in bed together."

17

I got to the Globe Hotel at eight-thirty the next morning, my head aching from lack of sleep and my eyes feeling as if tiny grains of sand were trapped under their lids. I was determined, however, to ignore my wretched state and get as much accomplished as possible before noon. Greg had said we would talk then about whether I would be allowed to continue my investigation, but I suspected that his decision would be a negative one. This morning might be my last chance to help my clients.

The lobby was deserted, and a hand-lettered sign on the elevator door said: *Out of Order.* Perhaps, I thought, last night's power failure had delivered it a *coup de grâce.* My weary body aching, I climbed the stairs to the fourth floor and knocked at the Vangs' apartment. Lan answered immediately, her face pasty, her eyes deeply shadowed. Her wan expression turned to relief when she saw me, and I realized that something was wrong here, something in addition to the events of the previous evening.

"Lan," I said, "what is it?"

"Please, come in." She opened the door wider and gestured with one arm.

I stepped into the living room, which looked dingy and ill-furnished in the subdued light that filtered in from the alley. The room was empty, but I could hear voices and the baby's cries from the adjoining bedrooms.

"What's happened?" I asked.

Lan glanced at the door to the bedrooms, then said in a low voice, "It is Duc. He did not come home all night."

"Has he ever done this before?"

"No, never."

"When did you last see him?"

"Before we left for the restaurant, at four yesterday afternoon. My husband had told Duc he might take the evening off from work, because of his grief for his friend. I thought he planned to stay here."

"When did you realize he was gone?"

"When the lights came back on after you and the policeman left. Before that there was such confusion, and Dolly needed me. I had no time to think of Duc. When I noticed he was missing, I did not mention it to anyone. I especially did not want my husband to know; he had had such a difficult day, so full of pain and shame for our daughter. But I lay awake listening for Duc until daybreak."

"Did you mention it to anyone this morning?"

"I have asked the other children. They know no more than I do."

"What about others in the hotel?"

"I asked Sallie Hyde and Mrs. Zemanek and several others. They had not seen him. I even spoke to the foot . . . beat officer. He said he could do nothing for seventy-two

132

hours, and then I must go to the police station and fill out a form."

"That's standard procedure here in missing person cases, unless there's some indication of suspicious circumstances. Duc is old enough to be out on his own, and there's no evidence he's been harmed."

"But he has never done this before!"

I patted her shoulder briefly, thinking of the talk I'd had with Duc yesterday. "Don't worry; I'll try to help you find him. What about his friends, the other boys? Did you question any of them?"

Lan brightened somewhat. "I had not thought of that. There is Hoa Dinh's brother, and the boys on floor five. Shall I go see them?"

"No, let me do it. I need to speak with them anyway, and I'd like to ask you to do something for me in the meantime." I got out the list of disturbances that Lan had given me at our first meeting and asked if she could fill in the approximate time of day each had happened. She said she would consult with the others, and then I left her and climbed to the sixth floor.

I was about to open the fire door there when I heard noises above. The door to the roof creaked on its hinges, then boomed shut. Footsteps sounded on the stairs, and seconds later Roy LaFond appeared on the landing. His mane of white hair was windblown and he was brushing dirt from his sharply creased tan slacks. When he saw me, his eyebrows shot up in surprise.

"Ms. McCone," he said in an obvious attempt to cover his confusion.

"Mr. LaFond, what a surprise. I thought you hardly ever came to the hotel."

"I don't, usually," he said, moving across the landing to the steps. "But with all these problems, I thought I should stop by and check things out."

"On the roof?"

He glanced back the way he had come. "On the roof, as well as in the rest of the building."

"And what did you find?"

"Nothing out of the ordinary. Now you'll have to excuse me. I have a meeting. . . ." He went down the stairs, and I listened to his footsteps clatter all the way to the bottom.

When I'd talked with him before, Roy LaFond had said he hadn't been to the hotel since last August. At the time I'd believed him; his manner had been convincing. But so had Otis Knox's—almost—until Knox had dropped his country-boy facade and shown himself for what he really was. As owner, LaFond would have a full set of keys to the hotel. There was nothing to prevent him from coming and going at will. But if he had done so often, wouldn't someone have seen him? That was another thing I'd have to ask people about.

I went through the fire door and knocked at the Dinhs' apartment, but got no answer. It was late enough that the family would all be off at their jobs. I got similar results at the apartments of Duc's other friends on the fifth floor, and made a mental note to come back later. Then I went downstairs, bypassing the Vangs' floor, to Mary Zemanek's apartment. The manager took almost a minute to answer, and when she saw me, her lips pursed in disapproval.

"You again," she said. "Now what?"

"I want to borrow your key to the roof."

"You've already been up there once."

"I want to go again."

"Well, you can't."

"Why not?"

"I don't have a key anymore." Now her mouth took on a sullen, downward slant.

"What happened to your key?"

"The owner took it. Said no one was to go up there again." She paused, then added grudgingly, "He's the owner. He has the right."

I watched her thoughtfully, then said, "I ran into Mr. LaFond in the stairwell. What was he doing here anyway?"

She bit her lip and her eyes strayed to the little Christmas tree. "That's none of your business."

"Well," I said, following her gaze, "at least he didn't make you remove the tree. Why did he go up on the roof?"

"I said, that's none of your business!"

The anger that lay under her defensive attitude didn't seem to be directed at me, however. On impulse, I said, "He didn't tell you, did he?"

"Tell me what?"

"What he was doing up there. You don't know any more than I do."

She drew herself up haughtily. "Mr. LaFond has no secrets from me." But the fury in her eyes told me I had been right.

I got the revised list from Lan Vang and checked it over. There was no pattern to the times of the disturbances—at least none that I could see. I'd have to examine it carefully later on, but right now I needed to go about the neighborhood while I was still able to investigate. After telling Lan I would keep asking about Duc, I went down the street to Hung Tran's grocery store.

The old man was behind the counter, wearing the same kind of gray smock and looking as if he hadn't moved in two days. He nodded politely when I came in, and didn't seem surprised when I asked how often he'd seen Roy LaFond visiting the Globe Hotel.

"At first, when he bought the building, it was often," he said. "Then not so much. Whenever he came he was with people who looked like real estate salesmen. I hear the building is for sale."

"That's true. When did you last see him?"

"Only a half hour or so ago."

"And before that?"

The grocer's eyes became veiled. "I do not remember."

"Mr. Tran, this is very important."

He looked at me for a moment, then seemed to make some sort of mental decision. "The day before yesterday."

"What time of day?"

"Late. It was dark. Perhaps after six. No later than nine. At nine my son comes to run the store until closing, and I go home. He does not like for me to be here so late."

And with good reason, I thought. Robberies—armed

135

ones—were common here in the late evening, and they could easily flare into fatal violence if there wasn't sufficient money in the till. I said, "What was Mr. LaFond doing at the hotel? Did you see him do anything unusual?"

Again his expression became vague. "He was there. That is all I can tell you."

"Can, or will?"

He gave me a politely inquiring look, pretending not to understand.

The grocer's silence didn't matter, though. What did was that I now had a witness who could place Roy LaFond at the hotel within a couple of hours of the time Hoa Dinh had died. Thinking of Hoa Dinh made me think of Duc, and I asked, "Do you know Duc Vang, Mr. Tran?"

Again he didn't seem surprised at my question. "Yes, the young man comes in here often. His mother has a young child, and she must work long hours at their restaurant. Duc helps her by doing the family grocery shopping."

"When was the last time you saw him?"

He considered. "Yesterday afternoon, perhaps at two o'clock. He purchased half a gallon of milk."

"And you haven't seen him since?"

"No."

"Mr. Tran, the other day I asked you about the *bui doi.*"

He nodded.

"Could either Hoa Dinh or Duc Vang be connected with them?"

"No. Most certainly not. The *bui doi* do not recruit young men of their type."

With his reply, I gave up any notion of a gang connection. "But Hoa and Duc and some others at the hotel were friends. You'd see them going about the neighborhood, wouldn't you?"

"Yes."

"What sort of things did they do together?"

Once more he put on his vague look.

"Mr. Tran, the reason I ask is that Duc Vang is missing and may be in danger. I need to know where he might go, what he might do."

136

"I see." Hung Tran folded his waxy hands across his smock and stared down at them for a moment. "You are a detective, are you not?"

"Yes," I said, puzzled.

"Well, that is what Duc and his friends fancied themselves to be. They went about the neighborhood being detectives. Actually what they did was more like spying."

"Who did they spy on?"

"Their families, particularly their sisters."

"But why?"

"The boys are very traditional. And they are afraid for their sisters in a neighborhood such as this. They wanted to make sure no harm came to them."

"And to make sure it didn't, they followed them?"

"Yes."

"Good Lord." That meant that Duc had probably followed Dolly on at least one occasion when she had met with Otis Knox. Perhaps he had even followed her to the Crystal Palace and figured out what was going on inside. What would Duc have done if he had known about Knox and his sister?

I thought I knew, and it made me even more concerned for the alienated and missing young man.

— 18 —

Brother Harry was preaching furiously in front of the Sensuous Showcase Theatre when I came out of the grocery store. He stood on his square of blue carpet, waving his arms and shouting and, for once, attracting quite a crowd. Behind him, the theatre was dark, although I could see the cashier just inside one of the plate-glass doors.

I went down there and worked my way into the crowd, curious to see what Harry was saying that had made them

137

stop. Up close, I saw that the preacher's fleshy face was a mottled red, his eyes flashing with zealous excitement. The intensity of his voice and motions seemed to hold his listeners spellbound.

"The wages of sin, brothers and sisters! The wages of sin is death! Otis Knox was a pariah among us, a panderer, a purveyor of sin and degradation! He has now been made to pay. . . ."

I looked around at the crowd. They were the usual neighborhood types—winos and bag ladies, pimps and whores, ordinary shabby citizens—and they all stared at Harry, mesmerized by his diatribe—which might very well be the only eulogy the porno king would ever have.

"The Lord has delivered a mighty blow and rid us of this foul creature! He has lifted His great sword and meted out His divine justice! Justice and retribution, brothers and sisters. Retribution for Otis Knox's sins. If you do not also wish to pay this same terrible price, you must repent. . . ."

I had heard enough. Turning away, I spotted Jimmy Milligan at the edge of the crowd. The poetry lover was obviously in one of his down periods, standing with his head bent, hands jammed in the pockets of his worn corduroy jacket. When I went up to him, I saw that he was crying.

"Jimmy," I said, "are you okay?"

He looked up, elfin face twisted, tears rolling unchecked down his cheeks. He said, " 'Come away, O human child . . . to the waters and the wild . . . with a faery, hand in hand . . . for the world's more full of weeping than you can understand.' "

"What is it, Jimmy?" I said.

He shook his head, tears flowing faster. " 'Come away, O human child.' "

I remembered that Knox had said Jimmy would sometimes stand in the street and cry. This was not unusual behavior for him and, at any rate, there was nothing I could do to help. I gave his arm an ineffectual pat, but he caught my hand and held on.

Through his sobs, he said, " 'The world's more full of weeping than you can understand.' "

I sighed and said, "I guess so, Jimmy." I stood there for a minute, holding his hand until he got himself under control. Then I watched him shuffle off down the sidewalk toward Market Street, still mumbling the poetic refrain.

The crowd around the preacher was beginning to thin. I skirted it and went up to the door of the theatre, where the cashier still stood watching through the glass, her jowly face rigid with revulsion. When I tapped on the door, she shook her head and motioned for me to go away.

I shook my head and indicated I needed to talk to her. Finally she unbolted the door and let me into the lobby.

"So what is it?" Her voice was harsh with emotion, and her eyes, beneath heavy blue shadow, were puffy.

"I need to talk to you about Mr. Knox."

"Talk to Brother Harry. He thinks he knows it all."

"I know how you feel; what he's doing is disgusting."

She clenched her teeth and glared out at him. "Yeah, it is! Otis never did a thing to him. Anybody else would have had the cops here every time Harry set up shop. But not Otis. Oh, he'd chase him off once in a while, but mostly he let him be. And this is how Harry repays him." Then she turned toward me. "So what do you want?"

"I'm a private detective, working with the police on Mr. Knox's death. I'd like to ask you a couple of questions."

She looked me over skeptically, but said, "So ask."

"I was with Mr. Knox at his ranch last night around seven-thirty. He got a phone call and indicated he needed to come back into the city. Do you know if anyone here at the theatre made that call?"

She shrugged. "I wasn't here then. I get off at six."

"Who was here?"

"Arnie, the projectionist. Karla, the night cashier."

"Where can I find them?"

"Karla's probably at home. I don't know the address off-hand, but I could look it up. Arnie's in the projection booth. He practically lives here, has a mattress in there where he curls up. Another of Otis's charities, like that fucking preacher."

"Where's the projection booth?"

139

"Through the door over there and up the stairs." She paused, then added in a small voice, "I don't know what to do."

"What do you mean?"

"About the theatre. Should I lock up and go home? I don't know what to do. I've been coming here every morning for years. There was always Otis to tell me what to do. Now I don't know."

Another of Knox's "charities" at loose ends. "Why don't you talk to Mr. Knox's lawyers?"

She nodded slowly, as if it were a revolutionary concept. "Maybe I will." And then she turned back to the door, one palm flat against the glass as she looked out at Brother Harry.

I went through the swinging door to the main part of the theatre. The big screen was dark, the rows of seats empty. To the right was a stairway that led up about six feet to a partially open door. As I climbed up, I caught the heavy odor of marijuana. I knocked on the door, and a voice called out for me to come in.

It was a small room, with a ratty mattress on the floor, rows of shelves that held film cannisters, and a projector positioned in the opening in the front wall. Arnie, the gangly youth I'd seen two days before in Knox's office, sat on a chair in the center, his feet propped on the table that held the projector, smoking a joint. His gaze wandered vaguely to my face, held there a few seconds, then slid away.

"Yeah?" he said.

"The cashier told me you might be able to answer a couple of questions."

"Sure."

"Last night Mr. Knox got a phone call at home around seven-thirty and had to come back to the city. Do you know if anyone here made the call?"

He sucked on the joint, held the smoke down, then expelled it slowly. "Yeah, me."

"Why?"

"Had to."

"Why?"

"Projector fucked up." He waved a languid arm at it. "I couldn't fix it. Tried. Couldn't. Customers walked out. Called Otis. He came in."

"And what happened?"

"He fixed it." Arnie held out the joint to me, and when I shook my head, he dragged on it again.

"What time did Mr. Knox get here?"

"Time?"

"Eight? Eight-thirty? Nine?"

"Maybe eight-thirty."

"And when did he leave?"

"After he fixed the projector."

I sighed. "How long did that take?"

"Not long. He's a smart man. Was. Could fix anything quick."

"Did it take fifteen minutes? Half an hour?"

"Half an hour max."

"And then what?"

Arnie crushed out the joint and laid it carefully on the edge of the table, then stood and went over to the projector. He touched the top reel with his index finger and spun it around. The film began to unroll.

"Arnie, what then?"

"He left."

"Do you know where he intended to go?"

"Home?" He spun the reel harder and film looped to the table. "Maybe not home. I don't know. I went outside with him. Needed some air."

No wonder you did, I thought, beginning to fear a contact high. "And?"

"And what?" He grabbed one of the loops of film and pulled at it.

"What happened when you went outside with him?"

"Oh, yeah. He went off toward that truck of his. It was parked in the passenger zone where he always leaves it."

"And then?"

"Harry stopped him." Arnie backed off from the projector, pulling the loop larger.

"The preacher?"

"Yeah, him."

"What happened then?"

"They talked."

"About what?"

"I don't know. I went back inside." The film snapped and Arnie began to unwind it from the reel.

"That's it?" I said.

"Yeah. Last I saw Otis, he was talking to Brother Harry."

The last I saw Arnie, as I hurried out of the booth, he was stringing film around like crepe paper at a child's birthday party.

The cashier wasn't in the lobby when I went out there, and Brother Harry and his audience had vanished from the sidewalk—probably the beat officer had broken up the gathering. I crossed to Knox's office and found the woman standing next to the desk, staring at the phone.

"I should call the lawyer," she said.

I nodded, looking around at the collection of memorabilia: the beer cans and mannequin limbs, the stolen highway signs, the fishnet with its shells, bobbers, and crutch. When acquiring them, Knox had probably never given any thought to the fact they might outlast him. Most of us didn't, as we bought an object here, picked up a treasure there. These things had had meaning for Knox; now they were merely fodder for the junkman.

The cashier was still staring at the phone. I sensed her reluctance to put an official end to her state of limbo. After a few seconds, I said, "How well did Mr. Knox know Brother Harry?"

She turned to me, seeming glad to have reason to delay her call. "Harry? Not well at all. You couldn't exactly say they had much in common."

"Did you ever see them talking together?"

"Trading insults, maybe, but not talking."

"Did the police run him off just now?"

"Yeah, even the cops can't stomach that kind of talk about a dead man. Actually the cops around here liked Otis. Didn't much care for his business, but they liked him personally."

"He could be charming," I said truthfully. "Look," I added, "would it be okay if I made a couple of local calls?"

"Sure, be my guest. Call long distance if you want. There's nobody to care now." She moved past me toward the door.

I sat down in Knox's chair, pulled the phone toward me, and called SFPD Homicide. When Greg finally came on the line, I told him about the projectionist's phone call and what he'd said about seeing Knox last with Brother Harry, as well as about Roy LaFond's undisclosed visit to the Globe Hotel. He took down the particulars, and then I said, "Have you gotten the autopsy results on Knox yet?"

"No."

"So you haven't formed an opinion as to whether it was an accident or murder?"

"Not yet."

"Have you had a chance to think about whether I can continue to work on this?"

There was a pause.

"Greg, I think I can help you. I know the people here; they trust me. Besides, there's been another development."

"What?"

"Duc Vang—the young man I told you about, who was so evasive about what he and his friends did in the neighborhood—is missing."

"Since when?"

"Sometime yesterday afternoon."

"So?"

I considered telling him about the boys' habit of following their sisters and my suspicions of Duc, but my loyalty to the Vang family—who were effectively my clients—prevented me. "He's never disappeared before. He may be in danger."

"Kids disappear in this city every day. If he doesn't turn

up by tomorrow, his parents should file a missing person report."

"Greg—"

"Sharon, how old is Duc?"

"I'd say in his early twenties."

"Then he's of legal age. And it's no crime for a person to be missing—you know that."

It was true. If Duc had chosen to disappear voluntarily, he was perfectly within his legal rights—provided he hadn't committed a crime. In fact, when the police located a missing adult and found he had disappeared of his own free will, they could not even report his whereabouts to those who had filed the report without his consent. But if a person were involved in a crime . . .

Greg said, "You'd better back off this investigation, Sharon."

I'd known he was going to say that, but I still felt a stab of dismay.

"Look," he went on, "I don't want you getting in our way. Besides, that's a dangerous neighborhood, and one person—maybe two—has already been murdered."

"You don't have to protect me."

"Heaven help me should I try. But I mean it—stay out of it. As a personal favor, I'll keep you posted on our progress, but that's it." He hung up to avoid further argument, and I sat holding the receiver, inwardly fuming.

Well, I'd predicted Greg's decision accurately, and now here I was at loose ends. I didn't dare go against his orders; I'd tried that in the past, when we'd been lovers, and had almost lost my license even then. So what to do now? Go back to All Souls, where there were documents waiting on my desk to be delivered and filed? They could wait until afternoon. Go home and check to see if Barry had shown up after I'd left this morning? Somehow I doubted he had, drunk as he'd sounded on the tape last night.

A dial tone was coming from the receiver. I reached over and punched Don's number on the pushbuttons. He answered, said Barry hadn't shown up at the house before he'd left, and asked if I wanted to have lunch.

"I've got to go downtown and pick up some new publicity stills at the photo processor's," he added. "Do you want to meet someplace near there? Temple Bar, maybe?"

The idea appealed to me. Temple Bar was a little hideaway at the end of an alley near Union Square. It was cozy and dark, and its gloom would match my mood. I told Don I'd meet him there at noon.

Then I thought of Carolyn Bui. She ought to know I'd been warned off the case. When I called her, however, she was just on her way out, to a meeting with one of their fundraisers downtown. On impulse, I invited her to meet Don and me for lunch.

It was only ten-thirty. I had an hour and a half to kill. Since I was going downtown, I could stop at the department stores and begin my Christmas shopping. Or . . .

Sallie Hyde's florist stand wasn't far from the restaurant where Don, Carolyn, and I were meeting. There was no reason I couldn't stop and talk with her. After all, what Greg had meant was for me to stay clear of the Tenderloin. Surely he couldn't object to me visiting an acquaintance at Union Square.

— 19 —

Last night's rain had completely blown over and once again Union Square sparkled with sunshine. Christmas shoppers were out in full force, as were the Salvation Army Santas and panhandlers. A string quartet in top hats and frock coats that made them look like characters out of Charles Dickens had replaced the dancer in front of I. Magnin's, and the strains of their carols mingled with the honk of horns and the shrill of traffic cops' whistles. Pedestrians crowded around the department store windows, pressing close to catch glimpses of the special holiday displays. I stopped to admire one myself—a Victorian parlor, complete with Christmas tree and automated figures of a family exchanging gifts.

Sallie Hyde was seated on the stool in her flower stand. She wore a bright red dress, but her big body slumped forward dejectedly against the little counter, hands idle, staring into space. The stand wasn't doing any business; people hurried by as if they were afraid they'd be contaminated by her aura of gloom. I made my way through the crosscurrents of shoppers, and when she didn't notice me standing there, I spoke her name.

Sallie turned and then her face pulled down in a scowl. "You!" she said.

It wasn't the reception I'd expected. "What did I do?"

"You know what you did."

"No, really I don't. What is it?"

Sallie looked away, and for a moment I thought she wasn't going to speak at all. When she did, her voice shook with anger. "You sent those cops after me. They came down here, asking me all kinds of questions, in front of my customers, even."

"Cops? What . . . ?" And then I remembered Greg had planned to run a check on Sallie. What he'd turned up about her prior murder conviction must have prompted him to send his men out to talk with her.

"Yeah, cops!" She turned on me, eyes flashing. "They come around asking me stuff like how do I feel about the Vietnamese who live at the hotel? Do I still have a problem with children? Where was I when the Dinh boy died? They did everything but accuse me!"

Abruptly her anger broke and she seemed on the verge of tears. "They come here to the place I work and ask me stuff like that when my customers are around. What if one of them heard and figured it out? They're my regular customers, they like me. What would they think if they knew? And it's your fault; you told them. I don't even know how you knew."

I *had* told Greg about Sallie's record, but I didn't see how she could be so sure of that. "Did they say I told them?"

She paused. "No. But you're the only one who could have. Nobody at the hotel knows. But you—you're a detective. You can smell out things like that."

I sighed. "All right, Sallie, I did tell the man in charge of the investigation. But they would have found out anyway. They run a computer check on anyone they interview, and that means all the residents of the hotel."

"But why did you *tell?*"

"Because I was more concerned about finding out who killed Hoa Dinh than I was about your feelings. I'm sorry it hurt you."

She looked at me for a moment, twisting a length of white corsage ribbon around her fingers. Finally she said, "You might as well sit down," and nodded brusquely at the other stool.

I sat, glad she'd accepted the apology.

"I shouldn't have gotten mad," she said. "I know past mistakes follow a person. But I was so young when it happened, in my early twenties. I was babysitting a relative's kid—"

"You don't have to tell me this."

"No, I want to. You see, I was angry about the babysitting. These relatives were visiting from Modesto, and everyone was off at a neighborhood street fair—this was in the Mission, back in the days when it used to be nice—but they left me to take care of the kid. Fat, plain Sallie—she didn't deserve to have any fun. Keep her at home where no one will see what a hog she is. That was the way they all treated me."

She pulled the ribbon tight until it bit into her pudgy fingers. "Anyway, the kid was just a baby in his crib. And all he did was scream. He yelled and yelled until I couldn't take it anymore, and I put a pillow over his face. I didn't mean to hurt him, but he was so little, and I didn't know my own strength." She was silent for a moment, staring down at her hands; then she looked up at me—timidly, as if she was afraid she'd disgusted me.

Carefully I said, "You were right in what you called it before—a mistake. A tragic mistake."

147

Relief spread over her fleshy features and she began to unwind the ribbon from her fingers. "It was tragic in a lot of ways. For the baby's parents. For my family. I lost them, you know; they never spoke to me again. I've lived in the Tenderloin for twenty-five years, ever since I got out of prison. I've got a brother across town in Noe Valley and a sister in Saint Francis Wood. Both of them have grown children I've never even seen. I paid for that mistake, I tell you. I paid."

"I know you did. We won't talk about it again."

She nodded and looked over her shoulder. A man in a Santa Claus suit stood there, a mixed bouquet in his hand, a concerned look on his face. He said, "Everything all right, Sallie?"

"Fine, Mr. Claus. My friend and I were just having a discussion about . . . someone who died." She got up and wrapped the bouquet for him.

When she sat down again, I said, "His name isn't really Mr. Claus, is it?"

She grinned. "No. It's Forbes. He's a retired actor, used to be big in Hollywood. Knew all the important people, went to all the fancy parties. But then he couldn't get work and was forced to come up here and live with his daughter. During the Christmas season, he's a Santa at Macy's."

I wondered how much of it was true, decided none of it but the Santa Claus part, and then decided it didn't matter anyway. Personally, I liked the idea of an out-of-work actor playing his yearly role as Santa, liked to think of old Mr. Forbes going to all those fancy parties with the important Hollywood crowd. Some people would call Sallie's imaginings lies; I called them her way of preserving her enthusiasm for life. And I sensed she only made things up about inessential matters. About those that counted, such as the questions I was about to ask her, she would be scrupulously truthful.

"Sallie," I said, "I came down here to ask you about Brother Harry, the street preacher."

"What about him?"

148

"Do you know if he ever had any dealings with Otis Knox?"

She considered. "Well, he's always on the corner in front of the theatre. He arrives in the morning and preaches until someone runs him off. And they don't keep him away for long. He goes and gets a sandwich or a cup of coffee and comes right back again."

"Is there any reason he chose that particular corner?"

"I guess the theatre. It's kind of an obvious example of what Harry hates."

"I wonder if there might be some less obvious reason. Did you ever see Harry with Otis Knox?"

"Only when they were hollering at each other on the street. Knox seemed to enjoy it as much as Harry."

"You never saw them talking?"

"Not that I recall."

"Does Harry talk to anyone in the neighborhood?"

"Anyone who will listen. But I don't call that talking; it's more like a harangue."

"About what?"

"Coming to God, what else?"

"Who *does* listen to Harry?"

"Nobody. But some people get buttonholed by him and put up with it for a while. That happened to the Vietnamese in our building when they first moved in. Even after they figured him out, they'd be polite. They're real well-mannered people. But when he started bothering the young girls, the parents got firm with him."

"Harry bothers young girls?"

My face must have reflected what I was thinking, because Sallie said, "Oh, not in *that* way. He just lectures them about stuff like their hair styles and tight jeans and makeup. The parents, including the Dinhs and the Vangs, went to Mary Zemanek and asked her to keep him out of the building. And they told the girls to avoid him on the street."

"Mary Zemanck really has her hands full, the way people can just walk into that lobby. Why don't they have a buzzer system?"

149

"Roy LaFond shell out for a buzzer system?"

I smiled. "I see what you mean." After a moment, I added, "Harry was preaching a sermon on Otis Knox's death this morning. It really upset the cashier at the theatre."

"Trust Harry to capitalize on someone else's tragedy." Sallie stood up, made change for a man who wanted a poinsettia plant, then returned. "I don't know what's wrong with that man," she went on. "He's so full of hate."

"Maybe it was something in his childhood."

"Yeah, that's the excuse they're always trying to make for the crazy ones." In better spirits now, Sallie dragged a bucket of red carnations over and began fashioning corsages. "But with me it doesn't wash. Harry's had a lot of years to get over his childhood, however bad it was. Look at me: I had a terrible early life, but I've made something of myself in spite of it."

"Yes, you have."

She grinned shyly at me. "Aw, you don't have to agree with me. I know a flower concession isn't much. But I work, I earn my keep, I've made a nice home for myself, even if it is in a Tenderloin hotel."

"That's better than a lot of your neighbors have done," I said absently, my mind still on Harry's choice of the corner in front of the Sensuous Showcase Theatre for his "church."

"I'll say. You know, when I was in prison I tried to educate myself. I took what classes were offered and got books from the library. I even tried to write."

"Really?"

"Yeah. I thought I would be good at it, on account of the way I like to make up stories about the people I meet. But somehow the words wouldn't string together right. What was in my mind wouldn't come out on paper."

"I know the feeling." Perhaps there *was* some hidden reason why Harry had chosen that corner. Some connection between him and Knox. . . .

"After I realized I wasn't going to be a writer, I decided

to try something more practical," Sallie went on. "Learn a skill so I could better myself when I was paroled. For a while I studied bookkeeping; a good bookkeeper can always get a job. But all those columns of numbers . . . and things never balanced."

"Sounds like my checkbook." Dammit, there *had* to be a connection somewhere.

"Trouble is, my teacher explained to me, I've got too much imagination. I'd be writing down the numbers and my mind would wander, and pretty soon I'd have left one out. So here I am, just an old flower seller, playing with roses to make ends meet." Sallie said it cheerfully, clearly content with her lot in life. Then she peered at my face. "You still troubling yourself about Harry?"

"Yes. I wish I knew more about him."

"I don't know who could tell you. There's a lot of people like him in the Tenderloin—myself included. We see each other every day, but nobody really knows anybody else. Maybe it's better that way."

"Maybe." I looked at my watch and saw it was time I went to meet Don and Carolyn.

As I stood up to go, Sallie plucked a yellow rose from a nearby bucket and pinned it to my lapel. "A peace offering," she said. "I'm sorry I hollered at you. Are we friends?"

"We're friends," I said—and meant it.

— 20 —

The Temple Bar was dark and crowded with people in business attire, drinking and talking while they waited for tables. I squeezed through them, murmuring apologies when I snagged my elbow on a woman's purse and banged into a man's briefcase. When I came in sight of the bar, I spotted Don hunched over a glass of red wine, in earnest conversation with the bartender. I went up behind him and touched his shoulder.

Don glanced at me and said to the bartender, "I'll give you a call."

The man nodded conspiratorially and moved away.

"What was that about?" I said as Don swung around on his stool to greet me.

"He's got a friend with a story I might want to use for a one-in-four."

"Graft and corruption in high places?"

"That's the right term for it—in high-rise construction. The bartender's friend is pissed off at a consortium of developers who ousted him, and he might be willing to rat on their connections with City Hall."

I smiled, marveling at how Don could walk into a bar, strike up a conversation with the barkeep, and come up with a possible story—all at the busy noon hour.

He said, "They're holding a table for us."

That was another of his rare talents—to have a table held while others stood in line. I said, "I hope there's room for three. After I talked to you, I asked Carolyn Bui to join us. You don't mind, do you?"

"Carolyn Bui—that's the Eurasian lady who hired you?"

"Yes."

"Great. I like her. She struck me as a pretty impressive woman, the way she handled herself after that mess last spring." He was referring to the case I'd been on when I'd met Carolyn.

"Yes, she is—" I broke off as I saw her emerging from the crowd behind us.

I reintroduced Don and Carolyn, and then we went to our table and ordered drinks. Deciding to get the bad news over with quickly, I told her about Greg ordering me off the case and Duc Vang's disappearance. Carolyn's face clouded and when the waiter set down her Campari and soda, she took a hefty sip of it.

"God," she said, "that family has been through so much!

152

I'll go by the hotel on the way back to the office and see if there's anything I can do for them. As for you, Sharon, it's too bad you can't follow up on this, but I understand why you don't want to put your license in jeopardy. I guess we'll just have to rely on San Francisco's finest." Her mouth twisted bitterly; Carolyn had had her fill of cops the previous spring.

The waiter came back and recited the specials. I debated the fish—red snapper—then opted for fettuccine with clam sauce. Don grinned knowingly; given the choice between something healthy and pasta, I'd pick the latter every time.

The sourdough bread wasn't fresh, since it was Wednesday, the day the bakeries were closed, but Don and Carolyn attacked it as if it were straight out of the oven. I toyed with a small piece, listening to him quiz her about the Refugee Assistance Center's programs. The dim light inside the restaurant did indeed match my dark mood, and the cheerful din of noontime voices around us only made me feel lower. Even the occasional touch of Don's hand on my arm didn't lift my spirits.

Our lunches came. I ordered another glass of wine—something I didn't usually do in the middle of the day—and pushed the fettuccine around, half-heartedly looking for the clams. Carolyn and Don were talking about the Hmong, the Laotian tribe without a written language. I tuned the conversation out and thought about Brother Harry.

I liked the idea that there might be some connection between the street preacher and Otis Knox, something that wasn't readily apparent to the casual observer. But how could I figure out what that connection was? The information I had on Harry was sparse, just that he lived in a flophouse on Turk Street and that his last name might be Woods. And those facts had come from Otis Knox; if he and Harry were involved in something—and knowing Knox, it would have been something less than legal—then he would not have told me the truth.

Of course I could try to get at the connection from another angle, by looking into Knox's life. But that would be risky, since the police would probably be doing the same thing. Still, there was nothing to keep me from hunting up a copy of that newspaper interview with Knox and reacquainting myself with the facts. And perhaps I could get hold of the reporter who had written it and quiz him about his impressions of the porno king. What was his name, anyway? Ellis? Yes, Jeff Ellis. He'd never returned the call I'd made the other day, nor had J. D. Smith. I should stop by the *Chronicle* building. . . .

"That's true," Carolyn was saying to Don. "Orange County is considered the leading center of Vietnamese life in this country. Specifically the stretch of Bolsa Avenue that passes through Garden Grove and Westminster—they have over two hundred Vietnamese shops and offices within a mile. But in Northern California, San Jose is beginning to rival that. There are over four hundred Vietnamese-owned businesses in Santa Clara County, and they also have the first refugee-owned commercial bank in Northern California."

Neither she nor Don seemed to have noticed my preoccupation, so I tuned out once again. It seemed trivial, discussing Chamber of Commerce statistics about the refugees when one of them had been brutally murdered and Duc was missing—or on the run. For that matter, my plan of talking to the *Chronicle* reporter seemed pretty trivial too. I didn't know for sure if Otis Knox's death was connected with either Hoa Dinh's murder or Duc's disappearance. In fact, I didn't even know for sure if Knox *had* been murdered. All this speculation about Brother Harry could be irrelevant. What mattered was Duc's whereabouts. Find Duc, and I could get the answers to quite a few questions.

Find Duc. What I needed was to take action, go out into the neighborhood and canvass the residents to see if any of them had seen him. If I talked to enough people, surely I'd find one who knew something. And if they were aware that Duc was missing, they'd be on the lookout for him. But I couldn't go back to the Tenderloin without risking a run-in with the police.

I pushed the fettuccine around some more, ate a clam, sipped wine. Carolyn was talking about her problems in getting funded; Don was properly sympathetic; my mind wandered back to Hoa Dinh.

What connection was there between Hoa and Duc and Otis Knox? What possible connection between two alienated young Vietnamese men and one of San Francisco's top pornography producers? Only Duc's sister. Duc might have killed Knox because of what he'd done to Dolly, but I couldn't believe he would have harmed his best friend. So maybe I was dealing with two killers. . . .

Dammit, I needed to get back out there and ask questions! And that was an impossibility.

". . . sounds like something I could do one of my one-in-four shows on," Don was saying. "This is an important issue here in the Bay Area, but I'm not sure how many people are aware of it. Our listeners should be informed about the impact the refugees are having on the city."

"What?" I said.

He smiled at me. "You're really not with us today, babe. I was just telling Carolyn I'd like to do a one-in-four on the refugee problem. What's going on now, what's likely to happen in the future, a little historical background—"

I stared at him. "What a terrific idea!"

He frowned, clearly puzzled. I was interested in his shows, but I usually didn't get this carried away over them.

"Don," I said, "today's Wednesday, the day of your talk show."

"Yes, we're running that tape of the Big Money Band—"

"It's not a one-in-four, then?"

"No."

"How flexible is KSUN about when you do them?"

"What do you mean?"

"Could you do a one-in-four tonight?"

"I suppose so." He glanced at Carolyn, who also looked puzzled. "There's no reason I have to use that particular tape. But I don't have anyone lined up for a one-in-four who could come in on this short notice."

"Yes, you do."

Suddenly Carolyn's eyes brightened, and she nodded, realizing what I was about to propose. Don continued to frown.

"Look, Don," I went on, "I was thinking just now about the missing man, Duc Vang, and how if people were aware of his disappearance, someone might come forward with a lead. Normally I'd go out and ask questions in the neighborhood, but I can't do it without getting in trouble with the police. But if we were to make people aware over the radio . . ."

He nodded, waiting.

"KSUN has a big audience in the Tenderloin—one of the women who lives at the Globe told me that, and I've heard it coming over radios in the stores down there. So I'm certain many of the refugees listen to it, and they'd be sure to pay special attention to a program about themselves."

"So what you're saying is that I should do a show in which I interview Carolyn about the refugee problem, and at the end she'd ask for information about this Duc Vang?"

"Yes."

"No." Carolyn leaned forward and put a hand on my arm. "Don can interview me about the refugees, but I think the plea for information should come from you."

"Me?" I said.

"Yes. A private detective would be more interesting to everyone. You'd really make them sit up and take notice. You could say you were working on this case, and then ask that people call in—"

"I couldn't!"

"Why not?"

"Go on the radio? Live?" My voice came out a high-pitched squeak, and both of them laughed.

"Seriously," I said, "I couldn't do it."

"Sure you could, babe," Don said.

"I'd be struck dumb."

"You? Never."

"Or die of sheer terror."

"This," Don said to Carolyn, "is a woman who has been known to pack a thirty-eight."

"That's different," I said.

"How?"

"Well, that's part of my job."

Carolyn said, "Then think of this radio show as part of your job, too."

I thought. My voice would quaver and crack; even if I wrote down what I wanted to say, I'd get it garbled; and afterwards I'd feel like running away to hide. But I guessed I could do it—for Duc, if for no other reason.

Then I thought of Greg Marcus. Was there any way he could accuse me of obstructing his investigation if I went on the air? No. How could he? He was the one who had told me the Vangs should wait until tomorrow before they even talked to the police. In Greg's eyes, Duc's disappearance had nothing to do with the cases he was working on.

"I'll do it," I said.

Don squeezed my hand.

"But *can* we do it?" I added. "Will the station allow it?"

His lips curved up slowly beneath his shaggy black mustache. "Of course."

"How can you be so sure?" Carolyn asked. "It's at the last minute—"

"Well, of course our program director, Tony Wilbur, will have the final say on that."

"Do you think he'll agree?"

"I know he will."

"How do you know?" I asked.

"Because," he said, drawing himself up proudly, "you are looking at the man who rescued a sodden and sloppy-drunk Tony Wilbur from jail the other night."

Of course—the Blue Lagoon fiasco. I said, "My mother always told me that a good deed never goes unrewarded. I'm finally beginning to believe her."

KSUN's studios were in a large white building that took up a square block on Army Street in the industrial Bayshore District. The building—rectangular, stark, and windowless —had no architectural merit whatsoever and would have blended in with the surrounding warehouses had it not been for the transmitting equipment and neon call letters on its roof. At seven that evening, the letters winked red against the dark sky.

I parked next to Don's Jaguar and went through the plate-glass doors to the lobby. Its walls were covered with plaques, framed awards, and publicity shots of the disc jockeys. Melissa, the night receptionist, sat at the desk, wearily leafing through a copy of *Variety*. When she saw me, she motioned at the door behind her and said, "Don's in Studio D. I'll buzz you in."

I'd been there many times before, so I knew to follow the hall straight ahead, past a big bulletin board that had all but disappeared under multiple layers of notices, schedules, posters of KSUN-sponsored events, ads for used merchandise, requests for apartments to rent, offers of free kittens, self-help workshops, exercise classes, guitar lessons, photography instruction, and low-cost psychotheraphy. One of Don's publicity stills hung there, and someone had drawn fangs and devil's horns on it.

At the end of the hall was a lounge with a couple of studios opening onto it. A red warning light shone above the door to the first one, and through its window I could see one of Don's fellow jocks putting a record onto a turntable while he spoke into the mike. Don and Carolyn sat on the broken-down couch in the lounge, going over a typed list of questions.

I greeted them, took off my jacket, and sat down in an

armchair that was even rattier than the one in my office. Then I looked around, wrinkling my nose in distaste. I am a reasonably tidy person, and from the first time I'd seen this lounge, I had wanted to attack it with a broom and mop. The shabby furniture and scuffed linoleum floor were always littered with rumpled sections of the daily newspapers; the low table in front of the couch held an assortment of empty pop cans, Styrofoam cups, overflowing ashtrays, discarded food containers, and scraps of paper. Right now there was a distinct odor of cigar, and a browning apple core crowned the heap in one ashtray.

"Okay," Don said to Carolyn, "that will do for your part of the show." Turning to me, he asked, "You nervous?"

"Me?" I held out my hands to show they were steady.

Don squeezed one and grinned when he felt how icy it was. "Relax," he said. "It's going to be fine. When we go on the air, you'll forget about all the people out there and just talk as if the three of us were sitting around chatting."

"Sure."

"Trust me."

He consulted the typed sheet, then said, "Carolyn and I have been talking about how we should structure the show. First I'll do a brief intro, asking Carolyn a few general questions, then lead into your case. You'll explain about it, make your plea for information about Duc, and while we're waiting for call-ins, Carolyn will discuss the Center and their work."

I nodded, liking the idea of getting my part over first.

Don stood up. "Let's go into the studio now so you can familiarize yourselves with it."

He led us into an unoccupied studio with a U-shaped console containing turntables, cassette players, a panel with dozens of buttons and switches, and a multiple-line phone. Behind the board—as the console was called—were shelves with racks of tapes, and to one side was a wall panel covered with gauges. Don showed Carolyn around, pointing out the equipment and talking about its functions, as he had the first time I'd visited the studio.

159

I stepped behind the board and sat in the operator's chair, my eyes drawn to the oscilloscope—a screen that looked like a target with moving green lines. Don had explained that it showed what the station's signal was doing—in a sense measured KSUN's pulse beat. He had also said it could be highly entertaining to watch on those occasions when a d.j. happened to smoke some of the grass that the engineer offered him during his long stint at the board. This unnamed engineer was also the one who brought in the beer and wine and hash brownies, and I found it interesting how the jocks' unprofessional lapses were always laid squarely at his door.

Off the main part of the studio was a booth measuring about four feet by ten feet, with a large window that overlooked the board. Don took us in there now. "This is where you'll be sitting during the show," he said. "I'll be out at the board, and we'll be able to communicate through these headsets." He indicated two pairs of heavy rubber earphones that lay on the table under the window, along with microphones with foam rubber tips and another multiple-line phone.

I put my purse on one of the straight-backed chairs and looked at the table, which was covered in carpet to muffle sound.

Don went on, "I'm afraid it'll get a little hot and stuffy in here once we're on the air." He grinned sheepishly and gestured at a vent in the accoustical-tiled wall. "We have a ventilation system, but it's so noisy we don't dare use it while we're broadcasting."

Carolyn said, "I guess Sharon and I are willing to suffer." She looked around, then motioned at a panel of colored lights next to the clock on the wall above the window. "What do these indicate?"

"They're the lights for the phones. The blue ones are outside lines—call-ins. Green ones are inside lines."

"And the red one?"

"In-house hot line. If it lights up, it probably means you've just said 'fuck' over the air, and the big boss is calling to schedule your execution by firing squad."

Carolyn laughed. I was too nervous to manage more than a feeble grin.

Don reached over and touched a small metal box that sat on the table. "This is the talk-back box. If you press the button, you can talk directly into my earphones through the mike. Use it if there's something you need to say to me that you don't want the listeners to hear."

"All right," Carolyn said. "So after Sharon makes her request for information, those phone lights will start flashing?"

"Hopefully. Sometimes it's a long wait. Fortunately, I can ask you questions in the meantime, so I won't have to ad-lib as much as normally. On one of my live shows a few months ago, no one called for what seemed like hours. I was yattering away, but none of the interviewees was responding, and I was running out of stuff to say. Everybody was getting nervous with all this potential dead air, and when one of the lines finally flashed, I pounced on it so fast that I scared the caller and he hung up."

Carolyn said, "Doesn't somebody screen the calls before you answer?"

"You mean, do we have phone clearers? No, and it's unusual. At most stations, the jocks don't pick up their own phones—they want to weed out the obvious crazies. But here at KSUN, we answer right off. I'm not so sure it's a good policy; the other afternoon I got an obscene drunk and I didn't bleep him fast enough. Still, for some unknown reason, management seems proud of not screening calls." Don shrugged and looked at his watch. "Fifteen minutes to air time. You know what you're going to say, babe?"

"Just what we discussed after lunch."

"Good. If you get nervous and feel your voice cracking or shaking, just take a couple of deep breaths. Don't be afraid of dead air; no one expects you to be perfect." He put an arm around me and gave me a brief hug.

I shook my head, amazed at his confidence. But then, I was pretty confident about tackling a tough witness or going into a risky situation in my own work. It was just professionalism, that was all.

Don had us sit down at the table and put the earphones on. He went back to the board, donned his own headset, and we went through the steps of talking back and forth, using the mikes, answering the phone. An engineer with long hair tied in a ponytail arrived—was he the one, I wondered, who corrupted the jocks with mind-altering substances? Soon it was only minutes to air time.

I glanced nervously at Carolyn, and she patted my arm, looking as miserable as I felt. My ears were beginning to sweat under the heavy rubber headset, and the booth was already stuffy and hot. When the light flashed indicating we were on the air, I controlled an urge to bolt from the studio.

Don began his intro to the show—cool and casual, sounding much more low-key than he did on what he referred to as his "daily screech and scream."

"Welcome to Don's Forum. For those of you who are hoping for something wild and wonderful, I've got to apologize. We did a serious one last week. Yeah, you remember the one on Golden Gate Park and the rising costs of keeping it green. Sure you do. No? Well, anyway, last week I promised you that tonight we'd wail. Really wail with the boys from the Big Money Band, in town for the Christmas show at the Cow Palace. Yeah, those boys are something!"

At that point he looked up and winked at me. Those boys sure were something—especially when taking an impromptu swim in the Blue Lagoon pool. I smiled back, thinking how different he was on the radio, even on this low-key show. The Don I knew was a man who used his words with economy; he would never chatter this way off the microphone.

"Really something," he said again. "And to prove it, they've waived air time tonight. Not permanently, mind you. But for tonight. Because tonight we've got two ladies here who have a real problem. And they want to talk to you about it. They think you may have a solution for them. I tell you, it's possible you could save a life. So stay tuned, and after this, we'll get into it."

He pressed the button on one of the cassette players and a commercial came on. Through my earphones, I heard him say, "See? Easy. When this is over, I'll introduce you, Carolyn."

Carolyn nodded and glanced at me, her face tense. My ears were sweating so badly that I reached into my purse for a Kleenex.

The commercial ended, and Don said, "Okay, here we go. With us tonight—and you folks out there better be with us too—is Carolyn Bui of the Refugee Assistance Center. Carolyn—let's be informal, huh, it's an informal crowd out there, but good guys, all of them, I can vouch for it—Carolyn, you want to tell us what the Center does?"

Carolyn cast a panicky look at me and then began to speak into the mike, her voice as cool and controlled as Don's. She explained briefly about the influx of Southeast Asian refugees, their needs for food, housing, and jobs, and the Center's role in helping them.

"But there are a lot of problems in our work, Don," she said. "It's hard to find places for the people. They don't have much money, and they need decent homes where they can bring up their kids."

"So you locate them in areas where rents are cheap?"

"Yes."

"And one of those areas is the Tenderloin?"

"Right. And you know, by and large it's been great. The people in the neighborhood have been very supportive. I think that a lot of them—particularly the older people, who have raised their own families and miss them—welcome the children. The children have given life to what used to be a dead place. They laugh, they play. . . . Well, you know what it's like to hear happy children at play."

"I sure do," Don said. "And I understand things were going well for your people in the Tenderloin until recently. But now there's trouble. Where did it start?"

"In the Globe Hotel. It's a nice apartment hotel, and even nicer since our people moved in and helped the other residents fix it up. We thought we were lucky, but then . . ." Carolyn's voice cracked and she looked at me.

"But then you were forced to hire a private detective," Don said smoothly. "And right now, folks, we'll leave Carolyn for a while and talk with that lady. Yes, that's right, she's a lady. Women can do anything these days, and Sharon McCone detects better than most. She's a staff investigator with All Souls Legal Cooperative out in Bernal Heights, and she's been in some tough spots in the past and knows her stuff. So let's have Sharon tell you about her case."

Until Don had said the words "private detective," I'd been caught up in Carolyn's seemingly effortless narrative. Now I was cold from nose to toes, in spite of the heat in the booth. Remembering Don's prior advice, I took a deep breath. Through the glass, Don was smiling at me. Carolyn's small hand pressed my arm. I made myself speak.

"Thanks, Don. I appreciate you saying I detect better than most, but right now I'm on a case that has me stumped. A couple of days ago Carolyn asked me to come to the Globe Hotel, and there I met a wonderful Vietnamese-American family, the Vangs. There are nine of them, and they live in a two-bedroom apartment. They own a restaurant—Lan's Garden, on Taylor Street—and everyone who is old enough works there. They are truly impressive people, the kind of people who built this country. And it's a further tribute to them that the other residents of the hotel nominated them to speak to me about the problem."

Don was smiling more broadly now. I must be doing okay.

I went on, "At first the problem seemed simple. Someone was frightening the kids in the stairwell. Growling at them. Howling. Silly stuff. The same thing was going on in the furnace room. And from time to time somebody would pull the main electrical switch and cause a power outage. I looked around but couldn't figure out who was doing it. But I assumed they would eventually give up if no one panicked."

164

Don said, "But then what happened, Sharon?" His face was glowing. I must be doing better than okay!

"A young man living at the hotel was murdered. His name was Hoa Dinh and he was sixteen years old. Hoa had come a long way from Vietnam, and he'd suffered a lot. But he'd made a new life for himself in this country, and then he died alone in a cold basement." I could hear emotion cracking my voice, feel Carolyn's fingers pressing tighter on my arm.

I took another deep breath before I went on. "But that's not the immediate problem. The police are working on Hoa's murder, and they will solve it." That was my sop to Greg, in case he found out about this broadcast. "The real problem right now concerns Hoa's best friend, Duc Vang. Duc—that's D-u-c—has been missing since yesterday afternoon. He's never done that before, and his family is afraid something has happened to him—something connected with this bad business at the hotel. And that's why we're talking to you. . . ." I faltered, uncertain how to address the faceless people, then seized on Don's term. "To all you folks out there. We need your help in locating Duc Vang."

Don cut in. "Can you describe him, Sharon?" He grinned, gave me a thumbs-up sign.

Damn, I *was* good!

I was so good I almost got carried away and forgot to answer him.

"Duc," I said, with a proper flash of humility, "is five-foot-six. He has black hair—a crewcut that is growing out. It looks brushy, stands up straight. He's slender and dresses in the old style, in a smock and loose pants. His mother says when she last saw him, he was wearing a blue smock and matching trousers. Oh, and he has a mole on his left cheek and likes to wear dark glasses."

I looked helplessly at Don, my earlier elation gone. He smiled, waited a couple of beats, then said, "So that's the problem, folks. The reason we're making you deal with se-rious stuff—that's spelled s-e-r-i-o-u-s—twice in a row. Sharon's a detective. Bona fide, card-carrying, tough. Believe me, folks, this lady is *tough*. But she can't figure it—Duc's disappearance. And she can't help him alone. Maybe you can help her. Come on, it's your turn to detect. Make like Sherlock Holmes. You never heard of him? What about Miss Marple? No? Maybe Sam Spade. Yeah!

"Anyway, folks, you want to help us? Maybe one of you has seen Duc, knows something about his whereabouts. You've got the description. You know as much as we do. You've got the number of the KSUN Hot Line. So let's get those calls coming *in!* Give us some *info,* ask us some *questions,* but *help us!* In case you don't remember, in San Francisco, the number's 752-7445. In the East Bay, call 845-5018. You folks down on the Peninsula . . ."

I expelled a breath and looked at Carolyn. She nodded, her eyes shining. Don finished and put on another tape of a commercial. Through the earphones, he said, "You guys were terrific."

I hit the talk-back button. "So were you."

"Thanks. When the tape's done, I'm back to you, Carolyn. I'll ask a question. You talk. Talk long, about whatever you want. The lines aren't exactly lighting up."

Both Carolyn and I leaned back, looking up at the lights above the window. They were dull and still.

Carolyn said, "Well, at least the in-house hot line isn't flashing. That means none of us said 'fuck.'"

Don laughed and said, "Commercial's almost over. We'll talk about general stuff. Fill lots and lots of air time until somebody gives us a break."

The commercial ended and he led into a discussion of the refugees: statistics, history, anecdotes. Carolyn talked, her eyes fixed—as mine were—on the lights.

"So what future do you see for the refugees, Carolyn?" Don said. "Where are they going in their—"

The first blue light started to flash. Carolyn's fingers dug into my arm. Don grinned in relief, picked up the phone, and said, "Hey, we've got a call-in. Don Del Boccio here."

"Don?" The voice was old-lady trembly.

"Yes, darlin'."

I started. It was a word Don never used, particularly to someone as old as this woman sounded. But this was radio, and when the woman replied, she seemed pleased.

"My name's Virginia Millburn. I don't know anything about the missing boy, but . . ."

"Yes, darlin'?"

"But . . . well . . . I *do* have a nice empty room in my house. A room with an adjoining bath. It isn't big, but I was thinking that if Carolyn had a small family or a couple who wouldn't mind sharing the kitchen with me. . . . Well, my husband died last spring, and I'd surely welcome some company. I wouldn't charge. The company would be enough, you understand."

Don blinked, obviously touched. "Virginia Millburn, you've made my day! Can you believe that, folks? This lady is offering to open her home to some of our new citizens. Virginia, tell you what—I'm going to switch you over to one of our KSUN operators and you can give him your name and address, phone number, all that stuff. And right after the show, Carolyn will be in touch. Hey, Carolyn— what do you have to say to this lady?"

Carolyn was shaking her head in amazement. "I say that's an incredibly generous offer. Thank you, Virginia. Thank you very much."

A second blue light had been flashing. Don switched over the call, then picked up the next line. "Don's Forum. Who's this?"

"This is Ellen. I think I saw the guy you're looking for."

I tensed; so did Carolyn; even Don's voice was taut. "Where, Ellen?"

"At the Greyhound bus station in El Cerrito. I recognized him by the haircut. And he had his guitar."

"His what?"

"His guitar." The words were slurred, and I realized the woman was either drunk or stoned. "Didn't you say he always carried a guitar?"

"No, darlin', we didn't. But thanks for the info. I want you to repeat it to our KSUN operator. So just wait a minute, I'll switch you over. Appreciate it very much." He looked at us and rolled his eyes. The other blue lights were flashing. He picked up another line. "Don's Forum. What have you got for us?"

The male voice was cultured and stuffy. "I must speak to Carolyn."

"You've got her." Don pointed at the phone in front of us.

Carolyn picked it up gingerly. "This is Carolyn."

"You're the Oriental lady?"

"Yes, I am."

"Well, why don't you and the rest of your people just go back to Japan?"

"What?"

"Go back to Japan where you belong."

"Sir, we're from Vietnam. We *can't* go back!"

"Just go back to Japan and take your Toyotas and Datsuns with you—"

The connection was abruptly broken. Smoothly, Don said, "A misunderstanding, folks. The fellow was obviously out at the fridge getting a beer when we got started." He picked up another line. "Don Del Boccio . . . I think."

"Hi, Don." The voice was deep and masculine. "This is Jim Wong. I've got a little house out in the Avenues, Twelfth Avenue, to be exact. I had a pretty good tenant there, but she moved out, and I was thinking. . . . The house is paid for and I don't need to charge a lot of rent. It's got two bedrooms, a big basement, a yard. Would be perfect for a family. Would Carolyn be interested in having it for some of her people? Say, for three hundred a month?"

Rents in the city for the kind of property he was describing started at around eight hundred. I looked at Carolyn; her eyes were wide.

"Carolyn," Don said, "would you be interested?"

"Would I? Mr. Wong, that's a most generous offer."

"Well," the man on the phone said, "it needs a new refrigerator, but I'm sure I could buy—"

"Mr. Wong," Don said, "*I'm* sure there's a listener out there who would provide a refrigerator. How about it, folks? Does somebody have an extra fridge? Just give us a call." Then he added, "Mr. Wong, I take it you're Oriental?"

"Yes, I am."

"Were you born in this country, or are you remembering hard times you yourself endured?"

The man laughed. "Buddy, I grew up in that house I'm offering out in the Avenues. I'm a native of the city, played football for S.F. State."

For the first time tonight, Don's composure was rattled. "*Football?*"

The man laughed harder. "You don't remember Crazy Jim Wong? My dad was Chinese, but my mother was Samoan. Three hundred and fifteen pounds now, some of it muscle, that's me!"

"Sorry, Jim," Don said, laughing himself. "I'm just a new kid in town. But I'd sure like to meet you sometime, and we really appreciate your offer. Will you leave your number with the operator?"

"Sure, buddy. And tell Miss Carolyn she's got a real sexy voice."

Lines were lighting up madly. Don picked up another. The voice at the other end said, "I want to talk to the lady detective."

Still glowing with pleasure from the previous call, Don said, "You've got her, guy."

Smiling, I picked up the phone and said, "This is the lady detective."

The voice was muffled, but I still could tell it was shaking with anger. It said, "The Vang family problem is not something you should interfere with. It is dangerous. You could die like the other one. Do not interfere with God's business. All things remain in God."

There was a click as he hung up. I sat there clutching the receiver, once again feeling cold all over.

— 22 —

Fortunately there were no more crank calls during the rest of the show. And once I recovered from the shock of hearing that hate-filled voice, I began to enjoy myself again. We received several offers of a refrigerator for Jim Wong's house, two more calls from landlords who were willing to rent cheap to refugee families, and seven highly dubious tips as to Duc's whereabouts. But the temperature of the little booth rose higher and higher, and both Carolyn and I heaved sighs of relief when we went off the air.

I yanked off my headset and stood up, running my fingers through my damp hair, and she did the same. Outside, Don pushed his chair back from the board and waved his clasped hands in a congratulatory salute. The engineer hurried out of the studio, and we trooped after him.

In the lounge, Carolyn turned to me, her face concerned. "Do you think that one caller was serious?"

"The religious nut? Probably not; most of them just like to hear themselves talk. Isn't that right, Don?"

"Yes. And the later at night it gets, the more they phone in. The worst slot I ever held as far as nut callers was midnight to four." But he looked thoughtfully at me; I'd told him about Brother Harry.

Carolyn shivered. "Still, it's scary knowing someone like that is out there listening."

I tried to make light of it. "It's also scary knowing someone wants you to take your Toyotas and go back to Japan."

She smiled weakly.

The engineer returned, bottle of wine and paper cups in hand. "Here," he said. "You look like you need this." He thrust them at Don, then went off down the hall, whistling.

I said, "That's the one, huh?"

"The one what?" Don sat down and began pouring wine.

170

"The engineer who gives you all the goodies."

"Oh, yeah, him and a couple of others."

"They *all* do that?"

"Most of them. Engineers are a weird bunch. But then, so are d.j.'s."

Don handed the cups around and we all drank in silence. After a little bit I said, "Will there be any more calls?"

"Probably not. But if there are, the operator will take them."

"I guess it didn't work—as far as finding Duc, that is. The other things should really help the Center."

Carolyn nodded.

"Unless," I added, "that crank call—mine—*was* from someone who knows something about Duc. Or about the murder. Maybe the show brought him out into the open after all."

"I hope not," Carolyn said. "That could be dangerous for you."

"Besides," Don said, "he's not really in the open. You still don't know who he is."

I sipped wine. "That's true. But I have a suspicion."

They both looked at me.

"I'm going to talk to the police about it," I added.

Don looked relieved. "You should. Why don't you use the phone in the studio?"

"No, I think I'll go back to All Souls." Frankly, I didn't want to talk with Greg in front of Don, even with a plate-glass window separating us. I didn't exactly know why, but it had something to do with keeping my past and my present segregated.

Carolyn finished her wine and stood up. "Well, I'd better get the phone numbers of the people who called in and call them back. I'm going to do it from home, though; I haven't been there for two days, except to change clothes."

"Reception will have what you need," Don said.

"Good." She looked at me. "Call anytime, if something comes up."

"I'll do that." I watched her leave, then turned to Don.

171

He said, "Are you really going to talk to the cops?"

"Of course."

"You're not going to go off on your own and get in trouble?"

He knew me too well. "No, I promise I won't. What are you planning to do now?"

"I promised one of the other jocks I'd help him edit a tape. I'll be here for a couple of hours, at any rate."

"Okay, I'll call you later and let you know what the cops said."

"Do that."

I gathered up my bag and jacket, gave Don a quick kiss, and went outside. The night was cold and crisp, and the Christmas decorations on the front door of the studios made me think—with a pang of guilt—of my undone shopping. But how could I worry about that until Duc was home safe and the murderer had been found? I couldn't; that was all there was to it.

I drove the short distance to Bernal Heights, realizing it would have been just as easy to go home and make my call. But somehow my house on Church Street—proud as I was of it—hadn't become home yet; I hadn't lived there long enough to really feel settled in. And All Souls had been my haven for years, the place where I'd always gone when troubled by the confusing and sometimes brutal reality I faced in my work. Even now, dead as the co-op seemed, it felt better to go there.

Surprisingly, warm lights blazed in the bay window of the big Victorian. I parked haphazardly and hurried up the steps into the front hall. A Christmas tree lay on its side in the archway to the left, and on the floor near the window a tree stand had been assembled. I looked around but saw no one.

Feeling a little more sanguine about the co-op—after all, someone had troubled to buy that tree—I went into my office and called SFPD Homicide. Greg was off duty. I tried his home number, and he answered on the first ring.

"Listen, Greg," I said, "I have a lead for you. I went on the radio tonight—"

"I know." His voice was grim.

"What?"

"A friend was listening to KSUN. He called me and said the lady I used to go with was on the air. Naturally, I tuned in."

"Well, then you know about the call I had—"

"Sharon, why are you interfering with my case?"

"I wasn't interfering. I barely mentioned the murder. What I was trying to do was draw attention to Duc Vang's disappearance—which everybody else seems to be ignoring."

"When a missing person report is filed and seventy-two hours have elapsed, it will get plenty of attention."

"Greg, that call—"

"That call could have been from any of the multitude of nuts who listen to the radio. A show like that brings them out of the woodwork. I don't want to hear any more about it."

"Greg—"

"And I don't want to hear any more from you either. As far as you are concerned, the case is closed. Do you understand?"

I didn't say anything.

"Do you understand?"

"Yes," I said sullenly.

"Good." He hung up.

I glared at the receiver, then slammed it into the cradle. *Why* had I ever thought Greg would be reasonable? I had a perfectly good lead for him—as I'd often had in the past. And he was going to ignore it—as he'd ignored other leads I'd given him over the years. And while he ignored it, Duc could be in even more serious danger than before.

Thanks to me. Maybe the broadcast had been a bad idea.

I shut off the light and left the office. I'd just reached the foot of the stairs to the living quarters when the front door burst open. Gilbert Thayer stood there, his bunny-rabbit face red and twitching. He looked around furiously, saw me, and said, "This is an outrage!"

I looked around too, but couldn't see anything that might

have upset him except the Christmas tree. "Why? We all enjoy a tree. Hank's Jewish, and he gets the biggest kick out of it of anyone—"

"Where is he? I'm not going to stand for this!"

There were footsteps on the stairs behind me. I turned and saw Hank descending, carrying a box labeled XMAS ORNAMENTS.

"Something the matter, Gilbert?" he said unconcernedly.

Gilbert raised his right fist and shook it. It clutched a piece of white paper that looked like an All Souls letterhead. "You'll never get away with this!"

Hank came the rest of the way down and set the box next to the tree. "Actually, I think I will."

"Never! You can't dissolve the partnership! Not without everyone's consent! And I'll never give mine! Neither will—"

Hank straightened, casually dusting off his hands. "Your trouble, Gilbert, is that you don't read carefully. Like you didn't read the regulation about who the driveway is reserved for. Probably that's what accounts for your mediocre grades in law school."

That stopped Gilbert, temporarily.

Hank went on, "You see, in our partnership agreement there's a provision for dissolution, as there is in all such agreements. And what it provides is that the partnership can be dissolved by a majority vote."

Gilbert's little eyes darted from right to left. Obviously he was calculating which partners would be for him and which against. I felt a bubble of glee rising inside me.

Hank said, "Don't bother to count. I've got the edge on you, by one person. The meeting that that letter informs you of will be held, the partnership will be dissolved, and the assets will be divided."

Gilbert's face began to twitch even more furiously. "The *assets?* What assets?"

Hank grinned. "Well, there's the office equipment— that's a damned good Selectric II Ted uses. File cabinets are kind of battered, furniture's not so hot, most of the

174

volumes in the law library belong to individuals. But there're some assets. There's the hundred-dollar cleaning deposit on the house—if anybody bothers to clean. There's goodwill, of course, and that entails use of the name. But you and your cohorts don't want the name, do you? Too sixties-ish, wasn't that what you said?"

He paused, looking elaborately thoughtful. "Oh, yes— there's the trophy we won two years ago in the ABA inter- city tennis tournament. It's kind of tacky, but it might fetch ten dollars. Of course, when you stack those assets up against the debts. . . . I'm not sure we've even paid the latest bill for stationery yet."

Gilbert balled up the letter he held and flung it on the floor. "You think you're clever, don't you?"

"Oh, moderately. More clever than you, perhaps."

"I want to see that clause in the partnership agreement." But the fight had gone out of Gilbert; already he was re- signing himself to defeat.

Hank extended his arm toward his office. "Sure. Come on and I'll show you. I happen to have a copy right on my desk." He winked at me and escorted the bunny rabbit down the hall.

I went over and picked up the letter, smoothing it out so I could read it. It was from Hank, in standard legalese, informing the partners of a meeting to be held at ten o'clock next Monday morning. The purpose of said meeting would be to take a vote on dissolving the partnership.

I smiled, willing to bet that Gilbert and his cronies were the only partners who had received copies of this letter. And I was also willing to bet there would be no dissolution, merely a few resignations and a quiet resolution of any re- maining problems. At the bottom of the page Hank had added a postscript that said, "Of course, All Souls has always operated informally. Should there be consensus in the interim between now and Monday morning that this time-consuming meeting is unnecessary, I am sure we will be able to dispense with it and get on with the more impor- tant work of this law firm—*namely, helping our clients.*"

I liked the italics. They were a nice touch. The letter had been typed and initialed by Ted, and he might even have suggested them, since his "damned good Selectric II" had an italicized element that he was very proud of. Yes, they were a nice touch indeed.

From Hank's office I could hear conversation. Gilbert's voice was subdued, a trifle whiny.

I started down the hall, smiling to myself. It was going to be all right. All Souls would survive, and probably be stronger for all this conflict. And my job would be secure. My job . . .

Halfway to the living room, I stopped, realizing I was still carrying the letter. Something made me look at it again, read it through carefully.

Those italics . . .

My smile became a frown, and I stood still for a minute or two, my thoughts in confusion, facts refusing to connect. Then I ran the rest of the way to the back of the house—and in a couple more minutes all the facts did connect.

I now knew where Duc was—and who had murdered his friend, Hoa Dinh.

— 23 —

Don said, "You'd better let me go with you."

I gripped the phone receiver harder. "No."

"Why not?"

"Because it's my job, not yours."

"But it might be dangerous—"

"No!"

My exasperation was apparent, and on the other end of the line, Don fell silent. He'd called All Souls just as I had been on my way out the door, hoping we could have a quiet drink or two. Instead I had presented him with the solution to a murder—possibly two—and a rescue plan. Now he was worried about my safety.

"Sharon," he said grimly, "go to the cops."

"I can't." But again I considered it. Maybe, given what I'd figured out, Greg would listen to me. If I called him back and explained. . . . But I knew Greg; he wouldn't listen. The only way to wrap this matter up was to free Duc. Greg couldn't refuse to hear *his* story. "I can't," I said again. "I'm counting on you to ensure that everything goes okay. If I don't call you in exactly an hour, I want you to call the cops. Tell them you want to report a homicide in progress and give them the address—"

"Homicide!"

"It's only a police code designation. It'll get them there in a hurry."

"Sharon, for God's sake, wait—"

"Remember, exactly an hour from now." I hung up and ran for the door.

I pulled my car close to the scaffolding that flanked the Crystal Palace Theatre and shut off the engine and the lights. I took my flashlight from my bag, checked to make sure the gun was secure in the side pocket, and got out of the car. The night was still clear and even colder; the outlines of the old theatre were more hard-edged than they'd seemed in the post-rain mist the night before. I looked up and down the street, saw no one, and ran for the opening in the scaffolding. When I reached it, I stopped, listening. I could hear nothing but muted traffic sounds.

The bare bulbs in the walkway beside the building were lit, and the narrow space was as eerie as a deserted stage set. Moving along close to the scaffolding, one hand holding the flashlight, the other poised above my gun, I approached the side door where Dolly and I had entered the night before. But when I tugged on the handle, it wouldn't open.

All right, I thought, this can't be the only entrance. The

177

theatre would have a stage door, closer to the rear. I retraced my steps, stopping at the opening in the scaffolding to look out. The street was still deserted. I went on about twenty feet, into the shadow where the light from the string of bulbs didn't reach, and found a small stairway that led up to another door. But when I climbed it and pulled on the knob, it wouldn't budge.

Of course after Otis Knox's murder—and now I was pretty sure it *had* been murder—the police would have secured the premises. But there must be another way in, one that hadn't been apparent to them. The person I was after had gotten inside many times, had taken Duc there. I'd continue to skirt the building until I found it.

This last section of walkway was very dark. I switched on the flashlight and heard a quick scurrying sound. Rats. The city had a problem with them; not so bad as a few years before, but still a problem. I swung the light around to further scare them, then edged along the wall toward the rear of the building.

It backed up on an alley where there was a loading dock. I boosted myself up on it and checked the door. It was the kind that raised up, and like the others it was secure. Sitting on the edge of the dock preparatory to jumping to the ground, I pondered the problem.

Was it possible, I wondered, that he had previously been getting in by one of these three doors that were now locked? One that had never been secured until after the murder? If so, it meant that Duc had been trapped in there for over twenty-four hours. Twenty-four hours without food or water, in a strange, dark place. I jumped down and continued my search.

Halfway along the back wall of the theatre, I noticed a window at ground level. It appeared to open into the basement where the dressing rooms were—and where Knox had planned to locate his sound stage. I knelt and examined it, found it was covered with heavy iron bars that were imbedded in the concrete frame. I shone the flashlight on the glass, but saw only the accumulated grime of decades.

There were similar windows all the way down the alley, and I checked each carefully. All were barred, all were dark and begrimed. Once again I retraced my steps, pausing beside a garbage dumpster and staring up at the brick wall of the building on the other side of the alley. The wall was honeycombed with windows, but none of them was lighted, and some were boarded up. Not a sound—not even the movement of rats—broke the stillness in the alley.

It was eerie being here in the heart of the city, yet so far removed from its life. Mere blocks away, people were swarming the streets and bars of the Tenderloin; a few blocks in the other direction, a different class of people were leaving the theatres, going to supper in elegant restaurants; and yards away, Duc was probably imprisoned, suffering . . .

I renewed my search, but with a feeling of hopelessness now, shining the flashlight's beam along the rear wall of the theatre. As it passed over each barred window, I noticed their even spacing and realized there should be another directly behind this dumpster.

The space between it and the wall was narrow, but I bent over and wriggled in. My jacket caught on the corner of the dumpster, and I yanked on it, felt it tear, and kept going. My flash showed me the outline of the window—a window similar to the others, except it had no bars. Squatting down, I turned the light on the frame and saw where they had been hacked away. There was no glass either, and a piece of plywood had been fitted to the frame. I touched it and it clattered to the floor inside.

I moved closer and thrust the upper part of my body through the hole, listening. No one came in response to the noise. In a few seconds I moved the beam of light downward. It showed a gray cement floor. Shining the beam around, I spotted three old-fashioned white porcelain sinks and a counter with a mirror above it. Obviously a dressing room. The distance from the window to the floor was only about seven feet.

I stuffed the flash into my pocket and slipped feet first

through the window, twisting around so I could grasp the sill with both hands. Then I let myself down and dropped to the floor. The air in there was damp and smelled of mildew. I listened again, heard no sound at all.

Taking the flashlight back out, I shone it around for a closer look. The counter extended along one wall of the room, the sinks along the other. There were hooks and mirrors on the walls, but otherwise no furnishings. A door led into what must be a hallway.

I went out there, listening once again, alert for even an intake of breath. The hall extended, black and silent, in both directions, and I turned right. A few doors opened off at intervals, and I looked cautiously through each. The rooms appeared to be dressing rooms like the one I'd entered through.

The air became chilly as I worked my way through the rabbit warren of little interconnecting hallways. At one point, two spiral iron staircases led up to what I supposed were the wings of the stage overhead. Then more hallways branched off, and more rooms. Several had rough plywood shelves—property rooms, most likely. Another had a counter opening into the hallway and clothes poles crisscrossed behind it—wardrobe. Still another seemed to have once been an office, with its old wooden file cabinets—which many an antique hound would have given his eye teeth for—still in place.

I kept turning down one or another hallway, unsure whether I'd been there before or not. My footsteps padded lightly on the concrete, my clothing rustled, but otherwise there was no sound. Even the street noises were stilled, and I felt that by descending into this concrete cavern, I'd left the city entirely, perhaps even moved back in time. But in another time, these corridors would have been filled with life, populated by brightly costumed performers—keyed-up, preening, anxious to go on stage. Now the theatre was still as death. . . .

As I neared the front of the building, I came to a large room with scenery flats stacked against its walls. I leaned against the doorframe, wondering what to do next. Duc wasn't being held in any of the dressing rooms; even if I wasn't certain I'd searched every one, this silence was so absolute that I knew no living thing shared it. There was no way Duc could have been present without me hearing a breath, a moan, a cry. Unless—

I started into the room, shining my flashlight on the flats that were stacked to the left. Then I turned its beam straight ahead and sucked in my breath. The flat against the far wall portrayed a barroom where shadowy figures sat drinking toasts, barely visible through what was supposed to be smoke-filled air.

It fit. It fit so perfectly that I hesitated to believe it.

I went up to the flat and tried to push it aside. It seemed solidly anchored. I ran around to the other end and tried to shove it in the opposite direction. It wouldn't budge. I grabbed it, pulled, and it came forward, revealing the outline of a door in the concrete wall.

The door appeared to have once been covered over with plaster-and-lathe, but that had been clumsily broken, ripped away. The plaster chunks and pieces of lathe were still on the floor, swept to one side. I stepped back and lowered the flat to the ground; a cloud of plaster dust rose to my nostrils.

This was what I'd been looking for.

The door, as well as the debris from the demolished wall, seemed to have been deliberately hidden behind the flat. By whom? Otis Knox? I didn't think so. He had mentioned his plan to get work crews in here, but not until next week. No, breaking through this wall was something that had been done without Knox's consent or knowledge.

I stepped over the corner of the flat and felt around the edges of the door. The space there was too narrow to get a grip on, but there was a hole where a knob had once been. I stuck my index finger into it and pulled. The door yielded with a faint squeak of protest. Ahead of me loomed a musty-smelling black space, and concrete stairs leading downward.

I trained the flashlight on the steps and went down them. The floor at the bottom was black tiles that looked to be imitation marble. It was very dark in there, and I raised the flashlight.

Directly ahead, maybe twenty feet away, was a heavy wooden bar, the kind that graced old-fashioned saloons. Its brass footrail flashed as I moved the light along it. Behind the bar was a mirrored wall, one large expanse of beveled glass surrounded by a grandiose carved frame. Bottles gleamed dustily on shelves that had been set up against the mirror—bottles that were draped in cobwebs and filled with the rich dark amber of whiskies and rums and brandies.

I swung the light to the right and saw small tables with chairs pushed neatly to them. The tables were topped in black marble and the chairs had seats padded in deep rose velvet. Against the walls beyond them were banquettes, upholstered in the same velvet. At intervals stood large pots that once might have held palms.

It was so nineteen-twenties, I thought. Secretive and exquisitely naughty. An intimate little place for people who wanted to engage in sophisticated, genteel, and illegal tippling.

The remoteness I'd felt before intensified as I stepped into this pocket of frozen time. San Francisco as I knew it ceased to exist. I could forget the eighties, the sixties, the year of my birth. They simply hadn't happened.

I'd found the rumored speakeasy, the one the owners of the Crystal Palace had tunneled out from the theatre during Prohibition. The reason it hadn't been discovered when work had been going on for BART and the Muni Metro was that it was under the sidewalk, not the street. The subsequent owners—including Otis Knox—had doubted its existence, but here it was. It had been waiting for decades in suspended animation, waiting to be rediscovered. And it had been—but not by me.

What had caused the owners to wall off the speak, leaving everything intact, every glass in its rack, chairs carefully pushed to the tables? The end of Prohibition, of course.

But why? Because they realized that the speak was no longer a profitable enterprise? Perhaps they'd left it this way as a bit of whimsy, a desire to preserve a relic of a soon-to-be-forgotten era. I would never know. . . .

I crossed the floor, swinging the light to one side, to an alcove that had probably been the checkroom. A cot stood there, a folding cot with a fluffy pillow and a striped olive-green spread. And olive-green sheets. Next to it was a wooden table that held an oil lamp, a transistor radio, and a stack of books.

I moved along the bar toward the alcove. Everything fit. Everything—

There was a faint groan behind me.

I whirled. "Duc?" I said.

The groan came again. I moved the beam over the wall next to the back bar. There was a door in it with heavy iron hinges. A storeroom? Refrigerated compartment? It didn't matter what. I ran over and tugged on the latch.

The heavy door swung toward me. Again I saw only blackness. Then I shone the flash down and saw Duc, lying on the floor, a cloth tied over his mouth, arms bound behind him. He rolled over, groaning louder now, and as I knelt, he looked up at me with imploring eyes.

"It's all right, Duc," I said, working at the tight knot in the cloth. "It's going to be all right; you're safe now."

Duc groaned louder. I dug my nails into the knot. One of them broke, but the knot held. Finally I yanked at the material. It tore, and I pulled it from Duc's face.

He drew in huge, gasping breaths while I attacked the rope that bound his wrists. His feet had been left free— there was no place he could go in this little storeroom. The rope was tied as tight as the cloth had been, and I finally pulled him into a semi-sitting position. "Just another couple of minutes," I said, "and I'll have you out of here."

Duc moistened his cracked lips. "Thank you." His voice rasped hoarsely.

Relieved that he was in good enough shape to speak, I said, "When did he bring you here?"

"He . . . I came myself."

183

The knot was a little looser now. "Why?"

"Dolly. After Dolly. I knew. I had seen. Before, I had seen." He paused, gasping. "I came downstairs. Down where they had been before. I looked, but there were only lights. They were not there."

"And then?" The knot was loosening, slowly.

"Then he—" Duc broke off, and I saw his sudden panic. His hoarse voice cried, "Look out!"

I let go of him and whirled around, reaching for my gun.

Jimmy Milligan stood in the doorway to the speakeasy.

— 24 —

Jimmy stood still, feet planted wide apart, hands balled into fists. The beam of my flashlight, reflected around the room by the dusty mirror behind the bar, showed his face to be more dismayed than angry.

I raised my gun and stood up slowly, putting a calming pressure on Duc's shoulder with my free hand.

Jimmy looked at the gun. His dismay turned to bewilderment, then fear. He raised his hands in a supplicating gesture and said, "'Cast a cold eye . . . on life, on death . . . horseman, pass by.'"

The words had to be from Yeats, and the response, like most of Jimmy's was slightly skewed. But now that I knew the poems he chose to recite were reflective in an oblique way of his reality, I could understand what he was saying.

I said gently, "It's all right, Jimmy. The dark horseman will pass by. I'm not going to kill you. Anymore than you were going to kill Duc."

His gaze moved to the young man on the floor. "'Come away, O human child . . . to the waters and the wild. . . .'"

184

It was the poem that had told me Jimmy had kidnapped Duc—Yeats' "The Stolen Child." He'd recited this refrain to me that morning while Brother Harry was ranting outside the Sensuous Showcase Theatre. And he'd been crying, probably because the kidnapping was an act he was ashamed of.

"'Come away—'" he said again.

"We'll come away, Jimmy," I said. "We'll all come away together. You, me, and Duc."

He looked back at me, his face calmer now. "Where?"

"Where would you like to go?"

"The lake isle of Innisfree?"

It was the title of another Yeats poem. "That sounds fine to me." I glanced at Duc. "Can you stand up?"

"Yes."

Still holding the gun on Jimmy, I helped Duc to his feet. He was unsteady and leaned against the edge of the bar for support.

"It's pretty there," Jimmy said.

"I'm sure it is."

"You can help me build my cabin of clay and wattles. I'll grow beans and keep bees. And be at peace."

"That's good, to be at peace." I wanted to keep him calm and talking until Duc could walk.

"Yes. We *can* be at peace at Innisfree. That's what Yeats said: 'And I shall have some peace there, for peace comes dropping slow.'"

"Then that's where we'll go—" I stopped, hearing a noise beyond the door to the speakeasy. It sounded like stealthy footsteps coming down one of the hallways.

Jimmy heard it too. His head snapped to the left and he tensed, listening.

The footsteps came into the room outside the door and stopped. It couldn't be the police; not enough time had gone by . . .

I stepped toward Jimmy, slowly. "Tell me more about the isle of Innisfree."

His panicky eyes moved back to me.

185

"Tell me, Jimmy. What was it Yeats said about peace?"

But he'd been brought back to reality by those footsteps. He made an inarticulate sound and whirled toward the door—just as a man blundered through it and down the stairs.

Don.

I wanted to scream at him. I wanted to hurl the gun at his head. Instead, I said, "It's okay, Jimmy. He's a friend—"

Don looked from me to Jimmy and back. I could tell he wasn't really taking in what was happening. Instinctively, he crouched, ready to spring at Jimmy.

Jimmy froze, then backed away. Don made a move toward him, and he growled like a cornered animal.

I said, "Don, for Christ's sake! It's all right!"

He looked at me, saw the gun, and relaxed slightly. The moment was all Jimmy needed; he bolted up the stairs and through the door.

I went after him, slamming into Don and falling against the steps. "Wait, Jimmy!" I shouted. "Wait!"

Don tried to get up the steps at the same time as I did, and he threw me off balance again.

"Dammit!" I said, pushing him furiously. "I told you to wait and call the cops!"

"I couldn't just sit there, knowing you might be in danger. . . ."

I scrambled up the stairs. Don came after me.

"Get out of here and call the cops!" I said.

"I'm not leaving you—"

"Go!" Far down one of the corridors, I could hear Jimmy's footsteps clanging on the risers of one of the spiral iron staircases to the stage wings. I raced along, following the sound. Don didn't come after me this time.

By the time I reached the staircase, I heard Jimmy's feet pounding hollowly on the stage above. I ran up the stairs, stumbling once and banging my shin on the metal tread. At the top, I was confronted by blackness. Standing there, I clutched the metal railing, waiting for my eyes to adjust. Somewhere in front of me and to my left, I heard Jimmy scrambling around, muttering inarticulately in a frightened, high-pitched voice.

Vague shapes began to emerge from the blackness, but nothing more. And my flashlight was on the floor of the speakeasy, where I'd set it before starting to untie Duc. I remained where I was, trying to visualize the layout of the stage as I'd seen it the night before. The stairway I'd run up came out in the right wing, where the players would wait to go on. The audience seating was to my right, backstage forward and to my left, where Jimmy was. He'd stopped moving now, but I could hear his labored, frightened breathing.

I said, "Jimmy, it's okay."

Even his breath stopped. Then it resumed, more quietly.

I closed my eyes—in spite of the fact they could see so little—and pictured the stage again. Somewhere behind me on the wall was the panel of light switches the police had used to illuminate the crime scene. I turned, hands out, walking blindly that way. In a few yards, my fingers encountered rough concrete. I moved to the left, then to the right, feeling the wall. Finally I touched electrical conduit, followed it to plywood, metal sheathing, and switches.

The night before the police had discovered that this board operated standard house lights rather than the footlights or colored stage lights that were anchored high up on the grid. They had had flashlights to guide them, however, while I could only rely on touch. I fumbled around, then grasped an unidentifiable switch and pulled. Nothing happened. I pulled a second switch, and the stage was bathed in a sudden glare. Now that I could see them, I yanked on all the others in order to light the entire theatre. Then I went after Jimmy.

He wasn't on the stage proper, so he must be somewhere behind the second set of heavy blue curtains, at the extreme rear where Otis Knox's body had lain. I grabbed their velvet folds, raising clouds of dust, and pulled on them until I found an opening. Then I burst through it, holding my gun in front of me.

The light back there was not as intense as on the stage. It

illuminated the scenery flats and ropes and metal supports I'd seen the night before. And the chalk marks where Knox's body had been. But there was no sign of Jimmy.

I was about to turn when I heard a whimper somewhere above me. Looking up, I spotted Jimmy near the top of one of the ladders to the catwalk.

He cried, "No!"

I said, "I won't hurt you, Jimmy."

He scrambled up on the catwalk.

I visualized Knox's body lying at the foot of that ladder, his neck bent at an odd angle. A shiver ran through me and I lowered my gun.

"Please come down," I called to Jimmy. "We have to go to the isle of Innisfree."

He hesitated a moment, but then began edging along the catwalk.

I set my gun on the floor where he could see it and stepped back. "Look, I'll leave the gun there. You can come down. We'll talk."

He stood still, staring down at me. I thought for a moment that I'd convinced him, but then he continued sidling along the narrow walk.

I took a deep breath and started toward the ladder. "All right, Jimmy," I said. "I'll come up there. Then we can talk."

No response.

"Jimmy, please wait."

All I heard was the metallic sound of his feet edging along the catwalk. The structure shuddered under his weight.

I reached the bottom of the ladder and grasped it, feeling the vibrations. But they didn't mean anything; it had been built to accommodate more than one person's weight, had probably been reinforced to comply with modern safety regulations; after all, hadn't Knox said they'd put on rock concerts here in the seventies?

I started climbing the ladder. Halfway to the catwalk I was tempted to look down at the stage. I didn't.

Near the last rung, my palms were sweating so badly that I almost lost my grip. I stopped, wiped one hand on my pants, got a firmer grip, then wiped the other. Finally I pulled myself up onto the catwalk and lay on my belly, listening to Jimmy's harsh breathing. I kept my eyes closed, telling myself not to think of the long drop to the stage. When I opened them at last, I saw the catwalk was wider than it had appeared from below—scant comfort, though, since the width was only three feet.

Finally I raised my head. The catwalk connected with the other ladder on the opposite side of the stage, the companion to the one I'd just climbed. Jimmy stood at its top, clinging to an upright support. It was shadowy up here, above the crisscrossed pipe of the lighting grid, so I couldn't see his face too well, but I could hear him crying.

Slowly I got up onto my knees, conscious of the catwalk's vibration. Jimmy whimpered with fear.

I said, "Aren't we going away together?"

He snuffled. "Not anymore."

"Why not?"

"I'm never going anywhere but down there." He jerked his chin at the stage below. "Just like Mr. Knox. I followed him up here and scared him, the way you're scaring me."

I eased back, sitting on my heels. "Why did Otis come up here, Jimmy?"

"I don't know. I came home and found him. He had all the lights on, and he was up here singing and laughing."

"Maybe he was happy because he'd bought the theatre."

Jimmy flinched and the catwalk shook with the motion. "He shouldn't have bought it! It was mine! It was my home!"

I said quickly, "I know. He had no right to invade your home. How long had you been living downstairs—in the place like in 'All Souls Night?'"

The mention of the poem seemed to calm him. "About two months. I figured out a long time ago how to get into the theatre. I borrowed a hacksaw and filed through the bars on that hidden window. I didn't mean to live here; the place was for sale and I knew they'd throw me out, like they did at all the other places I fixed up nice. All I wanted was somewhere I could be alone in the quiet."

Quiet. I couldn't hear a sound but his voice. Had Don called the police? Where were they?

I said, "But then you found All Souls Night."

"Yes. I'd heard there once was a speakeasy. It's an old story, and nobody believed it but me. But I had faith, and I found it. It was mine. It was home."

I waited a moment, then said, "Why don't we go back there?"

"No." He shook his head violently.

"Why not?"

"It's not my home anymore."

"Why?"

"Because everyone knows about it now. They'll take it away from me, just like all my other places. At first I thought it was going to be all right. The realtors came with lots of strangers. But they didn't know about All Souls Night, and I didn't mind them much. They never came back twice. But then one of them brought Mr. Knox. I liked Mr. Knox; he'd always been nice to me; but he kept coming back and coming back. Then he came without the realtor, carrying keys. And he had the electricity turned on. And he brought that girl."

"Dolly Vang."

"Yes." He bobbed his head up and down. I winced at the vibration his motions set up.

"And Dolly's brother and his friends followed them. That made even more people who came to the theatre."

"Yes, but they had been here before. They'd found my way into the basement and would come now and then to explore. I had to frighten them off. I had to defend my home."

"So you frightened them, by creating the disturbances at the Globe Hotel."

He clung to the support, looking down. "I thought if they had trouble there, they'd forget about this place."

"But they didn't."

"No."

"And you kept trying to frighten them."

"Yes."

"And the last time you tried, Hoa Dinh surprised you in the furnace room. And you hit him with something."

"A pipe that was there. I took it away with me and threw it in a sewer. I didn't mean to kill him; I was only defending myself." He began to sob again.

I heard the wail of a siren—muted but not far away. "Jimmy, let's go down to All Souls Night."

"No. It's not my home anymore."

I hesitated, then started moving slowly along the catwalk. "Jimmy, Duc's waiting there. He wants to go to the isle of Innisfree with us."

"He can't. Everybody's looking for him. You made sure of that on that radio show. I called, you know."

"I know." I kept inching along, not looking down.

"How can he go with us if everyone's looking for him?"

"We'll sneak away. They'll never know. We'll help you build your cabin and plant the beans—"

He raised his head and stared at me through the murky light. I stood still, not wanting to frighten him.

He said, "Yes, we'll plant the beans. And tend the bees. And when we're done we'll go out into the hazelwood and cut wands for our fishing poles. I did that once, you know. I went out and cut a wand and hooked a berry to it."

I realized Jimmy was paraphrasing his favorite poem, "The Song of Wandering Aengus," and felt a flash of relief. He was returning to his dream world—or maybe to his reality. I inched further along the catwalk toward him. "And then what did you do?"

"I waited until the moths and stars came out and then I went to the stream and fished."

"Did you catch anything?" I was only six feet from him.

Jimmy seemed as oblivious to my approach as he was to the dizzying drop to the stage. "Yes. A trout. A little silver trout."

191

There were noises in the lobby now. I tensed, but Jimmy kept staring out into the shadows, his eyes focused on his other world.

"And then what happened?" I was three feet away.

"She turned into a girl. A glimmering girl. She called my name. She ran away."

He was within reach. The noises below were louder.

"She had an apple blossom in her hair," Jimmy said.

I inched the remaining distance and grasped his arm, not hard. He looked at me in surprise and added, "I never found her again."

"Maybe you'll find her at the isle of Innisfree." I began moving him toward the ladder.

There were quick footsteps below us. Jimmy came out of his trance. His face went rigid with fright.

"What—?" he said.

There were police on the stage below us. I shouted, "It's all right! We're coming down. Don't do anything!"

Jimmy struggled against me, panicking. I gripped him with one hand, grasped the ladder with the other. The catwalk swayed violently. He was too strong for me. He would slip away and fall. We would both fall . . .

And then suddenly—just as in the grade-school spelling bees I'd always won—words appeared vividly in my mind. I said, "When we get to Innisfree, I want to go pick those silver apples. The golden apples too. The golden apples, Jimmy."

It cut into his panic long enough for me to tighten my hold on him. And once again it triggered a return to his other, gentler world. He looked at me for a moment and then said, "If you want to go with me, you'll have to get the words right."

I glanced anxiously down at the police, but they were waiting, weapons trained on us. "Recite them to me."

"'Though I am old with wandering . . . through hollow lands and hilly lands . . . I will find out where she has gone . . . and kiss her lips and take her hands. . . .'"

I urged him toward the ladder. Slowly he began to climb down, still speaking.

"'And walk among long dappled grass . . . and pluck, till time and times are done . . . the silver apples of the moon . . . the golden apples of the sun.'"

Wearily I started to climb down after him, my feet on the rungs his hands grasped. Jimmy fell silent, and I could think of nothing more to say. Halfway to the stage, his hand grabbed my right foot, and I fought off sudden panic. I pictured him yanking me from the ladder, and what it would be like to fall, screaming . . .

Jimmy said, "I never found her."

When I could speak, I said, "Maybe you will someday."

"No, we'll never get to the silver apples now. Or the golden apples. Or anyplace at all." And he let go of my foot and continued to climb down.

I kept going after him, on the verge of tears. Did any of us ever get to the silver apples, much less the golden ones? Did anyone, much less a lost soul like Jimmy?

When he got to the stage, Jimmy stumbled from the ladder, staring at the police in terror. I jumped down and stepped protectively between him and the armed men. When I took his hand, he looked down at me and said, "Did I tell you I once had a poem published? In a little magazine, but published nonetheless?"

I said, "Can you recite it for me?"

He paused and then looked over my shoulder at the waiting policemen. When his eyes came back to mine, they were sad and growing dull. "You know, I can't remember it. But what does it matter? Poetry's been my life's curse."

Then he raised his eyes once more, looked at the others, and said, "Can you imagine what it's like to have the soul of a poet in this world?"

I held Jimmy's hand all the time the police questioned him, until they had to take him away from me. And then I ran to Don, who was standing on the fringes of the crowd, and held him close.

Angry as I was with him, he was at least a silver apple—maybe even a golden one.

— 25 —

The city didn't look so bad from the roof of the Globe Hotel. Up there it was possible to pretend the squalor and ugliness in the streets below didn't exist. Temporarily, that was.

I stood by the cement parapet in the pale winter sunshine the Saturday after Jimmy Milligan had been arrested and looked out over the squat buildings of the Tenderloin to the graceful structures crowning Nob Hill. Then I turned and looked eastward, across roofs that stretched toward the industrial flatlands and the Bay. Somewhere over there was San Francisco General Hospital, where Jimmy was being held for psychiatric observation; if the people there were perceptive and really cared, he'd get the help he'd needed for a long time. Whatever the outcome, he'd have a permanent home, at the expense of the state. It was a great pity he'd had to kill to achieve that.

But this wasn't a time for gloomy speculations; around me the roof thronged with people. Roy LaFond was there, conferring with Lan Vang and Mrs. Dinh about what kind of soil and seeds and tools they'd need to start their garden in the new redwood planter boxes he'd had constructed. Don was running around with a tape recorder, gathering material for a follow-up show on the refugees. The Vang girls—even Dolly, who seemed to have recovered from the shock of Knox's death—clustered with others near the refreshment table, sipping sweet fruit punch and chattering about boys, clothes, and makeup—or whatever else American teenagers talked about. Even Duc, who had been uncommunicative for days, had come to the party. He sat on one of the lounge chairs LaFond had given the hotel, next to one of Hoa Dinh's brothers.

The owner had surprised me, surprised all of us except

Mary Zemanek, who had been in on his plans for a couple of days. It was he who had brought the live tree and ornaments to the lobby after hearing from me about the destruction of the Globe's Christmas tree—an act to which Jimmy Milligan had admitted. And the day I'd seen La-Fond coming down the stairs from the roof, he'd been measuring for the planter boxes. Mrs. Zemanek had been so outraged at his taking the key away from her that he'd had to bring her in on his plans to appease her. She was the one who'd suggested they give a Christmas party for the residents. Mary had prepared the refreshments; the food was courtesy of the grocer, Hung Tran; and the corsages and boutonnieres everyone wore had come from Sallie Hyde.

Now I turned and watched as Mary came through the door with a platter of cookies. She'd been grieving for days over Jimmy Milligan—and apparently had been worried about him before that, when she'd found the sack containing the olive-green sheet that I'd left in the lobby. She'd seen Jimmy washing his sheets at the nearby laundromat, and when I'd inquired after the sack, she'd begun to suspect that he might be involved in the disturbances, as well as Hoa Dinh's death. She looked reasonably cheerful today, though, and slapped at Sallie Hyde's hands when the fat woman grabbed a handful of cookies before the platter reached the table.

Sallie ambled over to me, held out her hand, and said, "Want one?"

I took a silver-sprinkled star, involuntarily thinking of Jimmy's silver apples. My expression gave me away, because Sallie said, "You still upset over Jimmy?"

"Yes."

"It's too bad about him. His craziness sure got out of hand. But maybe he'll be better off where he doesn't have to fend for himself."

"Maybe." I bit into the cookie, watching Jenny Vang chase her brother Billy around a potted fruit tree that stood near one of the planter boxes.

"The papers said you solved the case. They called it a

'literary puzzle,'" Sallie said. "Was that because of Jimmy's poetry?"

"Yes. Mary said something to me after Jimmy brought that ornament for the new tree—"

"Out of guilt for ripping mine apart, the swine!"

"Well, yes, out of guilt. Anyway, she said something to the effect that what Jimmy chose to recite reflected what was going on in his life. She mentioned his old favorite poem—'The Song of Wandering Aengus'—and how that was like his search for a home. And she also said he had a new favorite lately—'All Souls Night.'"

"So?" Sallie said around a mouthful of cookie.

"I didn't think much about it at the time, but I was interested enough in Jimmy to look at some of Yeats' poetry. I noticed he used a lot of italicized refrains, like a songwriter might. And I realized Jimmy had quoted some of them to me. But I still didn't connect him with the disturbances here or the murders or Duc's disappearance—in spite of knowing he sometimes did odd jobs around the hotel."

"Mary did hire him occasionally. He knew the place, and no one ever thought it odd, him being here. But what made you realize he was the one?"

"He phoned in to the radio show I was on. He disguised his voice, but he used one of the refrains from Yeats—*All things remain in God,* from 'Crazy Jane on God.' I still didn't connect it because it was religious and made me think of Brother Harry."

"That one! Did you know he got run in for disturbing the peace in front of the Sensuous Showcase last night?"

"No."

"Well, he did, and I hope he spends Christmas in the slammer where he can't ruin other people's enjoyment of it. But he'll be back; he always comes back." Sallie paused, looking censorious, then added, "You want another cookie?"

"I don't think so."

"Well, I'm getting some. And those brownies look good. Have a brownie."

Chocolate is one of my weaknesses. I said, "Okay," and watched her waddle to the table and load up a paper plate.

When she returned, she said, "I still don't understand how you connected it."

"Italics. I was looking at a letter where something was written in italics and that triggered an unconscious association. I looked up Yeats' poems again, and it was all there."

"Explain."

"First there were the words 'All things remain in God.' I knew it was Jimmy who had called me on the radio show then. Then there was the poem about wandering Aengus—like Mary said, Jimmy's search for a home. But he'd replaced it with a new favorite, which told me he might have found someplace to live. Everyone in the neighborhood who I'd talked to thought so, but no one knew where. So it had to be someplace very secret. The new poem, 'All Souls Night,' described something that might take place in an old, closed-up speakeasy like the one under the Crystal Palace."

"But how'd you know it was there?"

"I didn't, but Otis Knox had told me it might be, so I looked."

"And found Duc. How'd you know Jimmy had kidnapped him?"

"Right after Duc disappeared, Jimmy was very agitated and recited some lines to me, crying. They came from a poem called 'The Stolen Child.' When I finally put things together, I decided he had to have Duc imprisoned in the theatre."

"And Otis Knox?"

"The night he was killed, Jimmy was in a very manic state and quoting lines about death. They were appropriate to what had happened—too appropriate."

"Holy Jesus," Sallie said, "there were times when I was in prison that I thought I was going crazy. But I've never been *that* nuts."

"It happens, though," I said.

"I'll say." Sallie glanced longingly at the buffet table.

197

"Well, at least some good's come of all this. The owner's turned human. And speaking of the owner, here he comes." As LaFond approached us, Sallie escaped toward the food.

"A nice party Mary's throwing, isn't it?" he said, leaning against the parapet next to me.

"Very nice. But it wouldn't have happened without you giving her a reason."

He made a gesture of dismissal and looked fondly at his tenants, eyes crinkling at the corners against the wintry glare. "I wish I'd done something sooner. Never occurred to me. I was too wrapped up in my projects. But when you told me about their Christmas tree being ruined—well, that did something to me inside. You see, when I was a kid, we never could afford a tree."

So much for Carolyn's theory of LaFond as a spoiled rich brat, I thought. And, thinking of Carolyn, where was she? The party had been going on for over an hour and she still hadn't arrived.

"Of course," LaFond added, "I checked with my insurance broker. The additional premiums to cover people being up here on the roof aren't really all that expensive."

So much for my theory of LaFond as a complete altruist.

He paused, then said, "You didn't do too badly by these people either."

"It was my job to help them."

"But with you I sense it's more than just a job."

"You're probably right."

"You're like your friend Del Boccio. I can tell he also lives for his work."

"Yes, he does." I smiled fondly at Don, watching him interview Jenny—probably about what she wanted for Christmas.

"So now what?" LaFond asked. "Do you have other cases?"

"Not at the moment. I'm hoping to get my Christmas shopping done. And get my house in shape for when my brother and his kids come for the holidays." My brother

198

John was divorced and shared custody of their children with his ex-wife. She had wanted to go to Mexico for Christmas with her new boyfriend; he'd promised the kids a trip to San Francisco to see Aunt Sharon. I was actually looking forward to the excitement and upheaval, but it was going to be difficult having them there unless I got that bathroom finished. Barry the contractor had completely disappeared, leaving me with a pile of nails and a set of surgical tools I didn't know how to return.

I looked speculatively at LaFond. "Roy," I said, "you deal with a lot of contractors, don't you?"

"Sure."

"I have this problem with my house that you may be able to help me with. It involves hooking up a shower."

"Shower-tub combination?"

"Yes."

"Piping and drain in place?"

"Yes."

"No problem. I'll send someone out tomorrow."

"It'll have to be someone cheap. This project has been more expensive than I'd planned—"

"No charge."

"What!"

"Guy owes me a favor."

"Roy, I can't—"

"Take advantage of me while I'm feeling generous. Who knows—next month I'll probably come around badgering you to buy one of my condominiums."

"Well, thanks, then. I accept."

Suddenly the door to the roof opened and Carolyn tiptoed out, smiling mysteriously. When she came up to us, I said, "Where have you been?"

She put a finger to her lips. "It's a surprise. Watch the door."

I watched. In a moment, it burst open, and a hearty "ho-ho-ho" boomed out over the roof. Santa Claus—in the person of Mr. Forbes, Sallie's friend from Macy's—stepped out.

He bellowed, "Are there any good cl   here?"

Everyone on the roof turned—everyone except Sallie, who beamed proudly, watching their faces. Jenny stopped racing around the refreshment table and stood with her mouth open. Billy almost choked on a cookie. The teen-aged girls dropped their blasé poses and giggled. Even Duc smiled gently, as a murmur rose from both children and adults.

Santa said, "I've heard there are a lot of good children here." He lumbered over and sat on a lounge chair, opening the pillowcase that served as his sack.

Don came over and stood beside me. "This is terrific! What a great show it'll make, babe."

I nodded, watching Billy accept a package that looked to be the size of the toy truck his mother had said he wanted.

"Babe?" Don's voice was worried. "You're not still mad at me, are you?"

"No, I told you I wasn't. But in the future, you stick to radio and I'll stick to crime. No more heroics."

"It's a deal. Your kind of work is hard on a man's heart."

Or on a woman's, I thought, but not in the way you mean.

"Is Sharon McCone here?" Santa said.

I looked up, surprised.

"I hear you've been a good girl this year, Sharon. Come get your present."

I went over, took the gaily wrapped box he held out, and began opening it with eager fingers. The people clustered around me, watching. Inside was another box, and another, and another. The crowd laughed, and I unwrapped and un-wrapped. Finally I came to a cotton-swaddled object and unwound the white fluff.

Inside was a gold heart on a chain. It was inscribed "To Sharon McCone, from her friends at the Globe Hotel."

Tears stung my eyes, and to cover them I turned and hugged the nearest Vang daughter, Dolly.

Most of the time my work was bad for my heart, but there were also others when it was very, very good.